BOOTS & DIRTY TRICKS

UGLY STICK SALOON SERIES #6

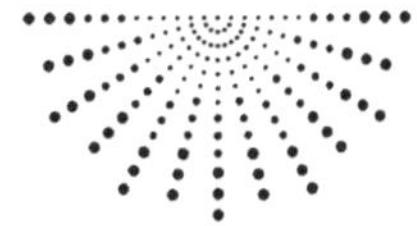

MYLA JACKSON

TWISTED PAGE INC

BOOTS & DIRTY TRICKS

UGLY STICK SALOON SERIES #6

New York Times & USA Today
Bestselling Author

ELLE JAMES

writing as

MYLA JACKSON

EBOOK ISBN: 978-1-62695-104-4

PRINT ISBN: 978-1-62695-105-1

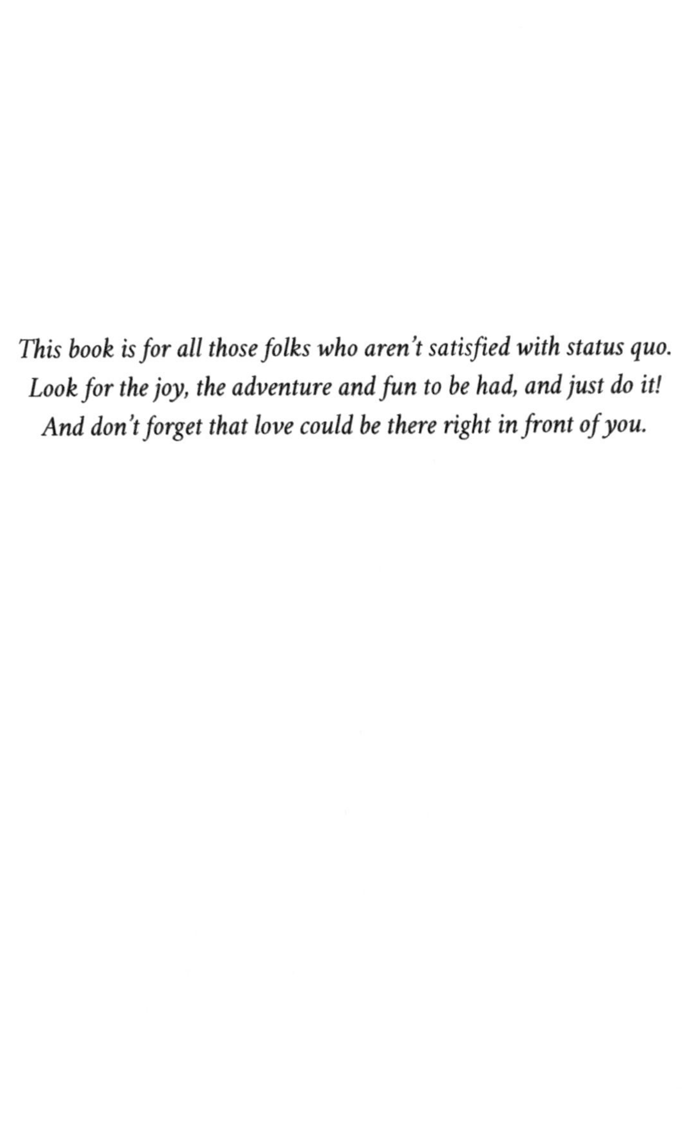

*This book is for all those folks who aren't satisfied with status quo.
Look for the joy, the adventure and fun to be had, and just do it!
And don't forget that love could be there right in front of you.*

Charli Sutton sighed and swiped the surface of the bar, her hand moving in slow, listless circles, her gaze following Kendall Mason and Ed Judson as they spun and laughed around the dance floor.

"What's wrong, Charli?" Audrey, the owner of the Ugly Stick Saloon, relieved Charli of the rag and tossed it into the sink behind the counter. "You haven't been yourself lately."

"I don't know." Charli heaved another sigh. "I think I'm missing Austin." She filled an order for a cowboy in a black T-shirt, sitting at a barstool and turned back to Audrey.

Audrey shook her head. "I don't miss Austin. That's where Randy and Jason live. I've never been happier getting as far away from the city as I could."

"Yeah, I don't miss them, but I miss the nightlife and the variety of people you met there. I've been here with you at the Ugly Stick from the start, but I'm...well..." She flung her hand in the air. "I don't know."

"Bored? Lonely? Need to get laid?" Audrey chuckled. "I can understand that. Been feeling a little that way myself."

"You?" Charli blinked hard and stared at her boss, noting

the beautiful strawberry blond hair and light blue eyes. "How could you be bored or lonely? You're gorgeous."

"And driven to make this place work. I don't have time to date. But you," she waived a hand in her direction, "have no excuse. You should be out there dating."

"Yeah, but it's been so long, what do I do? I'm starting to feel itchy. Wanderlust is tugging at me, making me want to leave or do something different." Charli pulled a beer mug from the shelf above her and filled it halfway from the tap, swallowing a healthy slug before she set it on the counter. The cool beer slid down her throat but did nothing to take the edge off her twitchiness.

"Are you unhappy being the assistant manager of the Ugly Stick?" Audrey asked.

"No, don't get me wrong." Charli leaned on the counter and sighed again. "I love my job."

Libby Hammons, with silky brown hair and deep cleavage flashing out of her low-cut blouse, slid her tray on the bar and offloaded the empties.

Even Libby managed to find dates in this little corner of Texas.

"Need 5 whiskey shooters, you choose the whiskey, a pitcher of Bud Light, a fruity wine cooler and five mugs for table twelve." She pushed her curly blond hair behind her ears and glanced over at Audrey. "I could use a hand with the tables in the far corner. Tia picked a bad night to be sick."

"I'll take care of them." Audrey grabbed an empty tray and hurried to the corner where the waiting customers were getting restless.

After Charli filled Libby's order and sent her on her way, she sighed for the hundredth time and slumped a hip against the bar.

"That's a mighty big sigh for such a pretty little lady."

Charli glanced at the man sliding onto the stool to her left. "What can I get you?"

"Guinness." He leaned both elbows on the counter, the movement stretching his blue chambray shirt over broad shoulders.

A tug of latent awareness pulled at Charli's gut. "Need a mug?"

"No, I like it straight from the bottle."

That tug blossomed into full-fledged attraction—the first she'd felt for a male in at least four months. Charli popped the top off the bottle and plunked it on the counter in front of the stranger. "You're not from around here, are you?"

"Actually, I am." He downed a healthy swallow and turned halfway around to watch the crowd on the dance floor.

Charli's brows dipped. "I haven't seen you in the saloon."

"Just back from a tour in Afghanistan. Before that, I was too busy preparing for deployment to stop in."

"Oh." Charli's interest perked and she looked closer. She should have known he was in the service. Hair cut short on the sides, his face angular, tanned and lean, the man reeked of military, his movements confident, strong and proud. Not a bad looking guy.

He faced her again, a smile lifting his lips, his teeth shining white in the semi-darkness of the saloon. "I'm Connor Mason, Kendall's older brother." He held out his hand.

Her brows lifted and she shook the man's hand, a jolt of awareness shimmying through her body. "Ah yes, Kendall talks about you all the time. Nice to finally meet you."

"I couldn't help but overhear your conversation with Audrey."

"It's nothin'". Charli shrugged. "I like moving around. I

grew up in a family that moved every two years. I'm hitting the two-year mark here."

"Thinkin' about leavin' then?" He swirled the beer in the bottle of Guinness, his attention there.

Not on Charli, as if he didn't really care what her answer was. A stab of disappointment made her reply short, "Yeah. I think so."

His chin came up and his lips twisted. "Be a cryin' shame. I was hoping to get to know you. To me, you're a fresh face to Hole In The Wall, Texas."

"Thanks, but I live in Temptation." The blue funk she was in lifted slightly, a glimmer of hope making her smile.

The cowboy in the black T-shirt lifted a finger to capture her attention. "Can I get another beer?"

Charli hurried toward him, anxious to take care of his order and get back to her conversation with Connor. "Another draft?"

"Yes, ma'am." His lips quirked up on the ends.

After filling his order, Charli hurried back Kendall's brother. She could imagine him in a uniform, her body warming all over. She loved a man in uniform. "How do people deal with nothing to do?"

"There's always something to do around here, you just gotta know how to make things happen."

"Maybe that's my problem. I don't know how." But she'd like it if he gave her a few ideas. She looked at him from beneath her eyelashes.

"You city folks are used to having everything at your fingertips."

"Are you slamming me for being a city girl?"

"No, not at all, just makin' a statement." He leaned forward, his lips turned up at one corner. "Out here, you gotta make your own fun."

"How?" Charli flung both hands in the air. "When people leave here, they go home. The Ugly Stick is where they go to make things happen. I work here. It's not the same."

Mason shrugged and took a long pull from his beer before he answered. "Guess it's up to you to figure out what's fun." He stood, slapped a couple bills on the counter, and tipped his fingers at her. "Nice to meet you," he said in his smooth southern drawl. Then he winked, nodded to the man in the black T-shirt, turned and left the bar.

Charli couldn't take her gaze off the man. Not until he disappeared through the entrance of the saloon did she realize her heartbeat had kicked up a notch. Not only that but she hadn't sighed in the past ten minutes, nor did she feel like it.

Connor Mason had her blood pumping like no other man had in the past two years since she'd been working the Ugly Stick.

With a lift in her step, she finished her shift, helped shut down the bar, slid into her black Mustang and pulled out of the parking lot. She lifted the hair from the back of her neck and let it fly in the wind from the open window. Before she'd gone more than thirty yards down the road, her cell phone rang on the seat beside her.

Now who the hell was calling her at three o'clock in the morning?

She glanced at the caller ID.

Blocked Sender.

She debated not answering, but after the fourth ring, she hit the talk button. "This is Charli."

"Ever skinny dipped in someone else's pool?"

Deep and masculine, the voice in the receiver was the kind that made coffee commercials sound sexy. It reached out to caress Charli's ear and other more easily aroused places of her body. A shiver of awareness snaked across her skin. "Who is this?"

"Let's just say I overheard your conversation at the bar."

Her breath catching in her throat, Charli clutched the phone tighter.

"You can spice things up if you dare," he said, his voice a sensuous whisper.

Charli tried hard to think who had been sitting at the bar that evening, only conjuring one image. That of the sexy soldier who'd blatantly eavesdropped on her conversation with Audrey. "Connor?"

"I'm not tellin'."

A surge of anger spiked her adrenaline. "Look, I don't need a pervert daring me to skinny dip in someone else's pool. Do me a favor and don't call this number again."

"With a body as beautiful as yours, I'm surprised you're afraid."

Charli's thumb hovered over the off button, but the deep timbre of his voice had her mesmerized, her body heating at the rich tone. "I'm not afraid. I'm just not stupid." She'd hoped to come off indignant, but the best she could do was breathless.

"Suit yourself and play it safe...or take the dare. Judge Stephen's pool, three fifteen—be there. I'll be watching."

A click followed by silence indicated he'd hung up. Charli stared down at the phone, not sure if she'd heard things. She shook her head. No, she had not just had a call from a sexy stranger daring her to skinny dip in the judge's pool. Temptation was too small a town. Getting caught wasn't a question. Everyone was always in everyone else's business. Besides, the judge lived smack-dab in the oldest neighborhood, surrounded by old biddies who spread gossip faster than a wildfire during a long Texas drought.

What was she even thinking about this challenge for anyway?

As her SUV drove past the turn to Judge Stephen's house, her foot slipped off the accelerator, her belly tightening.

She glanced at the clock on her dash. At three-twelve in the morning, all those old biddies were sound asleep. The judge would be as well. Her skin felt sticky from eight hours of work behind the bar and the hot Texas night wasn't helping to cool her. The thought of slipping naked into the cool waters of a swimming pool made her body yearn.

Before she could think a rational thought, her foot hit the brake, she spun the steering wheel and she slammed the accelerator to the floor, headed for the center of town. Two minutes until three-fifteen.

Mr. Sexy-Voice would be there watching.

CHAPTER TWO

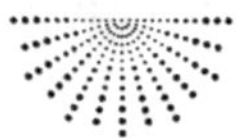

*C*HARLI SUTTON arrived for her shift early at the Ugly Stick Saloon, had the floors swept and mopped, the chairs arranged and the counters spic-and-span before her boss arrived.

When Audrey Anderson walked through the door lugging a box of whiskey, she whistled and her brows rose. "I believe a mystery elf has been at work here."

Charli eased down off the ladder she'd climbed to clean the old-fashioned mirror spanning the wall behind the bar. "I had energy to burn, I thought I'd get started early."

Audrey frowned, waving a hand at the bar's interior. "You did all this? I'd say you had energy. Did you sleep here?"

"No, of course not." With a laugh, Charli relieved Audrey of her box and hurried toward the storeroom behind the bar. She'd barely slept all night.

Audrey followed her into the storeroom and leaned against the door. "Okay, spill. Who are you and where did you hide Charli?"

"I *am* Charli. The same Charli you've seen here every day for the past two years." Charli smiled and shifted from one foot to the other, wanting to divulge her secret but afraid her boss would think her crazy. She wasn't ready to share what had happened the night before. Not yet. When she'd woken this morning, she'd pinched herself, wondering if the previous night hadn't been one elaborate and very sexy dream.

The ache between her legs and the rawness of her pussy reminded her the escapade had not been her imagination. She really had been naughty with a stranger. Not only had she made love to someone she didn't know, she'd done it in the judge's swimming pool. And, if she was not mistaken, the judge had been watching.

A shiver of excitement rippled across her body and moisture pooled between her legs. All of her newfound excitement was due to a whispered dare from the man in the black cowboy hat. He'd been at the bar the night before, watching her...listening to her conversation with Audrey about being bored with life in Temptation, Texas.

She thought she could name all the regular customers in the bar. Was the cowboy who'd fucked her in the judge's pool been one of those men she saw on a regular basis? Had she underestimated someone?

Audrey crossed both arms over her chest. "I'm not letting you out of here until you tell me what's going on." Her eyes narrowed.

"Nothing's going on." Her gaze shifted high and left. She'd always been a terrible liar. "Come on, Audrey, we have work to do. The bar opens in—"

"Thirty minutes. You have everything done." Audrey's eyes narrowed even more until she was squinting at Charli. "Something's different. You got laid, didn't you?" Her frown cleared and a smile lit her face.

Heat spread from Charli's chest up into her neck and face.

Ah hell, not only was she a terrible liar, she'd never been good at hiding her feelings.

"You did. I knew it." Audrey grabbed Charli's hands and dragged her into the bar, pushing her onto a padded stool. "Tell all."

Charli laughed, the eruption of sound ending on a sigh. "There's not a whole lot to tell."

"Start from when you left the bar and don't leave out any of the details. I want them all." Audrey sat on a nearby barstool and propped her chin on a fist, her eyes wide, eager.

Shifting in her seat, Charli glanced away. The excitement of the night before rippled through all over again. "Well, when I left here, I got a phone call from a man daring me to skinny dip in Judge Stephen's pool."

"What?" Audrey sat up straight, palms flat against her knees. "You didn't take the dare, did you? They call Judge Stephens the hangin' judge for a reason."

Charli shrugged, her lips twisting into a wry grin. "Yeah, well...I did."

"Skinny dip?" Audrey let out a long low whistle and grinned. "Baby, I didn't know you had it in you. Go on."

"Anyway, the guy who dared me said he'd be watching."

"That's it? Just watching?" Her brows wrinkled. "I thought you got laid."

Charli's lips twitched. A shiver ran through her at the memory. "Oh, he didn't just watch."

"He joined you?"

"And how." With another sigh, Charli leaned her elbow on the counter and stared across the deserted dance floor, last night's scene replaying across her mind. "It was magical...floating in the water, being touched...made love to...Sheer magic."

Audrey sighed as well, her eyes glazing. "Nice." She blinked and straightened. "Okay, who is the lucky fella?"

The images disappeared like a popped bubble. "That's the problem." Charli's arm dropped to the counter. "I don't know."

"You don't know?" Audrey stood. "You had sex with a guy and you don't know who it is? What did he look like?"

Charli shrugged. "Tall, dark, built like a fortress."

"Hair, eyes? What color?"

"I don't know." She shook her head, her words lame even to her own ears.

"How could you not know?"

"He wore a black cowboy hat pushed down low over his eyes. I couldn't make out his facial features in the shadows."

"What about his hair?"

"Same. The hat hid hair and eyes."

"Holy crap, Charli. What were you thinking?"

Her stomach curled into a ball. What had she been thinking? "That there was moonlight, the night was fabulous and filled with stars." Charli jumped up from the stool and paced the length of the bar, turned and paced back. "I got excited and suddenly he was there. It felt right. Hell, this vagina hadn't had any action in nearly six months."

"He could be a pervert, a serial rapist or worse...married!" Audrey flung both hands in the air. "Haven't I taught you any better?"

"Hey." Her body went rigid. "Weren't you the one telling me I should take a chance?"

"A chance on a guy you know, not a mass murderer."

"You don't know that he's a murderer." Charli stepped behind the counter, grabbed a rag and scrubbed the counter.

Audrey laid a hand over Charli's, halting her frenetic cleaning spree. "You don't know anything about this guy."

"He was here last night. He overheard our conversation." She looked into her boss's eyes. "Shit, Audrey, he has to be one of our customers."

"It was Friday freakin' night. We always have a lot of customers on Friday nights—married and single. You can't know everyone. It had to be someone sitting close to where you were." Audrey squeezed the bridge of her nose between her thumb and forefinger. "Who was sitting at the counter last night?"

"God, it was so busy, I can't remember." Charli recalled the guy with the military haircut. "Kendall Mason's brother. He had a stool at the counter last night. He even made a comment about making any place fun, if you try."

"Connor Mason?"

"Yeah, Connor." Charli's heart skipped several beats. Connor was tall, built Army-tough and incredibly sexy in that I-eat-bullets-for-breakfast way. Her eyes widened. "You think he might have been the guy who dared me to swim in the judge's pool?"

Audrey frowned. "He just got back from Afghanistan." She touched a finger to her chin. "Maybe. No telling. Hell, fourteen months in a war zone without sex..." Her hair bobbed as she nodded. "Was he wearing or carrying a black cowboy hat?"

Charli's shoulders drooped. "No."

"Don't rule him out. He could have had it in his car or truck." Audrey checked her watch. "Do you think whoever it was will show up tonight?" She looked up, connected with Charli's gaze and nodded. "Duh, of course you do, or you wouldn't have been here an hour early. Speaking of early, we better unlock the doors. The after-work crowd will be arriving soon."

Charli let out a relieved breath, glad Audrey would focus on something other than Charli's love-life.

Halfway to the front entrance, Audrey spun and shook a finger at Charli. "Don't think you're getting off light. I'm watching you and I'll be looking for anyone in a black cowboy hat tonight. And no more dares!"

Charli held up her hands in surrender. "No worries, I've learned my lesson. Never make love to a stranger in a black cowboy hat." A chuckle rose up in her chest, a smile spreading across her face. "I'll get his name first."

Audrey rolled her eyes, turned and unlocked the entrance.

Several men spilled inside, laughing, calling out to each other, their boots scuffing across the floor.

Her gaze on every man passing through the door, Charli searched for a black cowboy hat. Plenty of straw hats and a few ragged baseball caps drifted by, clutched in hands or perched on a head, but no black cowboy hat. With Saturday nights every bit as busy as Fridays, Charli didn't get much of a chance to study all the men in the bar.

Between slinging bottles like a pro and satisfying drink orders for the very busy waitresses, she didn't have the opportunity to talk to the men filling the bar stools more than to give them the drinks they ordered. She knew two of the eight men personally, the other four were repeat customers she hadn't had the time to get to know. Connor Mason wasn't one of the men leaning on the bar, sipping beer and talking.

Audrey joined her briefly after ten when the band took a break and everyone rushed to the bar for a refill. "See him yet?"

"I told you, I don't know for sure who *HE* is."

"Connor Mason." She tossed a bottle of scotch in the air,

expertly caught it and poured a jigger into the glass in front of her tipping it up with a flourishing wave of her hand. She set down the scotch bottle, grabbed the water nozzle and topped off the glass. "Did you see Connor?"

"No." Charlie jammed a pitcher beneath a beer tap and flipped the spigot. She grabbed two bottles of Guinness, tossed them in the air, caught them, popped their tops and slapped them on Libby's tray, completing the order with the full pitcher of beer. "He's not here as far as I can tell."

Audrey frowned. "Who else?" As she dragged a bottle of tequila over five shot glasses, she glanced fleetingly at the crowd. "Geez, what's the occasion? We're never quite this busy on a Saturday night."

"Rodeo weekend." Charli popped the cork on a wine bottle and tipped it into a long-stemmed glass.

"Think your cowboy is with the rodeo?"

Charli stared through the crowd, her gut clenching, praying her black-hatted cowboy was with the rodeo. Bronc riders never stuck around. "God, I hope not."

"Yeah, they leave all too soon." Audrey gave her a quick hug. "How about the guy at the end of the bar, he's staring at you like he wants you."

"That's Jackson Gray Wolf, Audrey. And he's staring at you. If he was staring at me, it would be because I still haven't gotten his beer to him." Although Charli wouldn't mind doing it with Jackson, he'd had his eye on Audrey since she took over the Ugly Stick Saloon. Only Audrey didn't have time for a love-life. "Why don't you go for him?"

"Who? Jackson?" Audrey hefted the tray she'd filled with ten drinks onto her shoulder and stepped out into the crush. "No time for love, sweetie. No time for love." Audrey disappeared into the crowd of cowboys and cowgirls, a sea of denim and belt buckles, and all there to have a good time.

Kendall Mason slapped her tray on the counter and plunked her butt in a seat vacated recently by a cowboy. "Remind me to wear tennis shoes next time I work."

Guilt causing her heart to thump against her ribcage, Charli grabbed empty glasses and mugs from the tray and dropped them into the soapy water of the sink behind the bar. "How's school?"

"I graduate in just under a month. Can't wait." She whooshed out a long breath. "Then maybe I'll get a real job."

"And make a lot less money."

Kendall sighed. "Yeah, but at least I won't have to work nights and weekends. I've got a real, honest-to-goodness sex-life now. I want to live it."

"Point made." Charli couldn't help the nudge of envy. "How are things between you and Ed?"

"Best sex ever." She grinned. "What about you? Dating anyone?"

Charli's lips pressed together. "No." Not really. How could she say she was dating someone if she didn't know who it was or if it would ever happen again?

"You should." Kendall gave Charli her order and stood waiting, her gaze staring out across the ocean of faces. "Love is wonderful."

"I wouldn't know," Charli said, her voice flat, unemotional. "Say, didn't I see your brother last night? Is he back for good?"

"Connor?" Kendall's face brightened. "Oh, yeah. Isn't it great? He's back from the war early. It's so good to have him home safe and in one piece."

"Is he here tonight?" She fought to keep interest from her voice.

"Not that I know of. I left him playing cards with Ed. The

two are buds from high school. They have a lot of catching up to do."

Charli's shoulders slumped. So much for a repeat performance of last night. If her man in the black hat was in fact Connor Mason.

With Connor out of the equation, Charli took more interest in the other men at the bar, staring at their builds, imagining them naked and partially submerged in water.

A couple of the guys seated at the counter could be broad shouldered and tall enough to be her mystery lover. A thrill of lust gripped her body, sending waves of sensation through her, reawakening her core.

One of the men lifted a hand to get her attention.

Her stomach knotting, Charli walked toward him, thinking the whole way, *This could be him.*

As she came abreast of the cowboy, she forced a smile to her face, praying her lips wouldn't tremble…unless of course they looked sexy trembling. "What can I get you?" she asked, her voice cracking, so unsexy-like.

"I'm good, it's just…" He crooked his finger.

Heart racing, Charli leaned closer. "Just what?"

"You have cherry juice on your…" He reached out, his finger nearly touching her breast when he pulled it back, his eyes widening. "Er…on your…there."

Her pussy creaming, Charli nearly fell over the counter into his dark brown eyes. "What?" she asked, completely oblivious to the shouts and noises surrounding her.

"You have a red juice streak on your…you know."

Charli's gaze dipped to where the man pointed. On the swell of her breast was a long pink, sticky trail of cherry juice. Heat rushed to fill her cheeks. "Oh. Well." She dabbed at it with a cocktail napkin but the sticky juice didn't wipe clean.

"Here, let me." He dipped a napkin in a full glass of water and leaned over the counter, his darkly tanned face within inches of hers, his full, sensuous lips curled in a hint of a smile.

Rooted to the spot, Charli couldn't move, her breath catching in her throat, butterflies flapping against the inside of her belly. A waft of leather and soap drifted her way, further scrambling her brain cells.

The cowboy pressed the icy-cold, wet napkin to the swell of her heated breast.

Her knees threatened to buckle, her vision blurred and she thought she might pass out.

"Breathe," he whispered into her ear. "I won't bite you...unless you want me to."

Charli's eyes widened and she remembered to fill her lungs. More warmth flooded her cheeks and she fought to keep from leaning into him to steal a much-desired kiss. "I'm not afraid of you. It's just that the water is cold."

As he rubbed the napkin across her breast, her nipples beaded, making distinct points jutting through the thin lace of her bra to make twin bumps on the front of her ribbed knit white tank-top.

The cowboy's gaze dropped lower, the grin widening. "How long is your shift?"

"I close the bar." A hint of disappointment filled her. Her mystery lover knew she closed the bar. He'd waited until she had finished her shift and called her when she'd been on her way home. He must have been watching for when she left the Ugly Stick Saloon.

Too bad. This guy was cute. By the size of the ridge pushing against his fly, he was well equipped, like the man who'd come to her in the judge's pool.

"I can hang around." He sat back on his stool and lifted his beer mug. "I don't know many people in this area."

"Oh, yeah?" That made two of them. "Just visiting?"

He nodded. "Staying with a buddy of mine from the Army."

Her pulse picking up, she leaned across the counter. "Connor Mason?"

"Yeah, you know him?"

"Met him last night." She glanced over the stranger's shoulder, her gaze scanning the bar's patrons. "Is he here?"

"Said he'd be here after he ran an errand."

Libby and Audrey swung by with empty mugs and orders to fill. Charli took care of their requirements and saw to her other customers at the bar before returning to Connor's pal. "Got a name?"

"Guess it would only be polite to exchange names, considering I've already touched your breast." He laughed. "Name's Reed Townsend."

Her skin tingling where he'd touched it, Charli held out her hand. He engulfed it in a large grip, equally strong and gentle. "Charli Sutton. Nice to meet you."

"Charli, I need two shooters and another pitcher of beer." Libby plunked her tray on the counter and off-loaded the empties.

Twenty drink orders later, Charli swiped the back of her hand over her forehead and turned to the bar stool where Reed had been sitting, a smile on her face.

Reed was gone. In his place was a middle-aged farmer with a beer gut the size of a keg.

A quick scan of the busy bar yielded neither hide nor hair of Reed, Connor or anyone else remotely resembling her cowboy in the black hat. Charli sighed.

The rest of the night dragged on, Charli serving one

drink after the other in an endless flow of alcohol. As three o'clock approached, her heartbeat kicked into overdrive. She couldn't clear the drunks out of the building fast enough. What if her cowboy in the black hat called and suggested another tryst? Maybe a sexy detour on her way home, a dirty trick to be played out naked and with a lot of heavy breathing.

"Are you feeling all right?" Audrey approached with a tub of dirty glasses and plates. "Your face is kind of flushed." She set her tub on the counter and reached out to press the back of her hand to Charli's cheek.

"I'm fine, just working hard."

"Let me close up tonight. You go on home and get some rest." Audrey took the rag from Charli. "Go on." She shooed Charli with a wave of her hands.

"Okay, okay." Charli grabbed her purse from under the counter and ducked into the bathroom to run some cool water over her face, fluff her hair and stare dismally into the mirror. Not like that little bit of primping improved her work-weary appearance. She sighed, hiked her purse up on her shoulder and headed out the back door.

"Get some rest," Audrey called out as the door swung closed behind her. "Or not..."

Charli's gaze panned the back lot behind the bar. Only her SUV and Audrey's bright red pickup remained. No other cars or trucks waited. As she pulled around to the front, only one lonely car was left parked in the lot. Probably someone who'd hooked up with another customer. The lucky dog.

Her phone sitting beside her in the console, Charli pulled out on the road, her body tense, her hearing tuned in, waiting for the call. As she neared the exact spot where she'd received the call last night, her breath caught in her throat and she couldn't resist glancing down at the phone in the cup holder, her foot lifting from the accelerator.

Ring.

The spot on the road came and went, the phone remained silent. Charli grabbed it and checked to make sure she'd left it on. Her screensaver lit, displaying a picture of bluebonnets beside a country road. It appeared to be functioning. Maybe the ringer had stopped working. Maybe, she'd gone through a dead-zone of cell towers.

Maybe he wasn't going to call.

Her heart grew heavier the closer she got to Temptation. So much for a repeat performance of last night. What did she expect? A man who pursued her every night until he had her so worked up she couldn't function?

She loosened her grasp on the steering wheel and rolled her shoulders.

Get a grip. Men in black cowboy hats didn't just appear out of thin air. Perhaps last night had all been a dream. A damned good wet dream. Her pussy clenched, just thinking about how he'd fucked her, her body caressed by the warm water of the judge's pool. The added excitement of potentially getting caught making the experience all the more enticing. What were the chances of recapturing such a night, much less topping it?

The miles passed and Charli resigned herself to going home to be alone. Unfulfilled, and no more knowledgeable about her cowboy than the night before.

As she rounded a curve in the road, two sets of headlights flashed in her eyes, a blue light flashed over the top of them. Charli slammed her foot to the brake, screeching her SUV to a stop just in time to keep from hitting the two vehicles completely blocking both sides of the road.

Raising a hand to shield her eyes from the overwhelming

brightness, Charli shifted into park and waited. Sometimes the state troopers performed road blocks on weekend nights to check for drug-runners, human-trafficking or drunk drivers. She'd heard about road blocks, but had never been caught in one of them.

A tall figure approached the side of her vehicle, wearing a dark cowboy hat, dark jeans and a black shirt.

Her heart leaped into her throat and the fingers curled around the steering wheel tightened. She drew in a deep breath and berated herself for even thinking about her cowboy when this patrolman was only out doing is job. Letting out the breath, she reached for the button to roll down the window. "What seems to be the problem?"

The lights behind him cast the man's face in the shadows. "Ma'am, please step out of your vehicle."

At that point, she noticed he wasn't wearing a badge or any other insignia proclaiming his connection with law enforcement. And that voice... The man's deep, rich tone sparked fire in Charli's blood and memories of last night. Her heart raced and she fought to form coherent words. "Am I being accused of something?"

"No, ma'am. Just routine orders," he said.

That bottomless, soul-melting voice flowed over her like liquid chocolate. The same voice she'd heard on the phone and in the pool the night before.

"We're here to search everyone passing on this road."

Search? The very word brought to mind endless possibilities. "Could you show me some credentials?" Her breath hitched in her chest, her body heating. It was him—her cowboy in the black hat. She peered upward, unable to make out his facial features. Damn. If she could see his identification, she might put a name to this man. "How do I know you are who you say you are?"

He reached into his back pocket, removed his wallet and flipped it open and closed in a flash. "Satisfied?"

"Hardly." She wouldn't be satisfied until she knew who he was and got a little more of what she'd received in the pool the previous night.

"Now, if you'll please step out of the car, my partner and I will get down to business."

Her hand on the door handle, she hesitated, her pulse pounding. "Partner?"

Another man, also wearing a black cowboy hat, stepped up to her door, grabbed the handle and pulled it open. "Yes, ma'am. If you'll step out of the vehicle, we can conduct this search and get you off in no time."

The second man was equally as tall and as broad-shouldered as her cowboy from the night before. A shiver of need whizzed across Charli's skin. Two cowboys? Was she dreaming again? Wasn't it every girl's fantasy to have two hunky cowboys at one time? Or was it only in her perverted mind?

Despite the inner warnings going off in her head, she couldn't stop herself from stepping out of the SUV. As soon as her feet touched the ground, she was yanked into the first cowboy's arms, kissed soundly, then spun away and pushed up against the hood of her vehicle.

Surprise had her reaching out to stop herself from crashing into the metal. Cool handcuffs snapped onto one wrist and then the other before she could protest. With her hands bound together, she tried to push away from the SUV and stand straight. "Hey, what's with the cuffs?"

"Routine, ma'am." Her cowboy leaned over her shoulder, his breath stirring the tendrils of hair over her ear. "Now spread your legs." He braced one of his boots between her feet and kicked her right foot outward.

Forced to spread them, Charli's belly tightened, her pulse racing. "What are you going to do?"

"We have to search you."

"For what?" she asked.

"For a few minutes. Now silence or we'll be forced to perform a strip search."

"Oh, boys, I don't think you know quite what you're doing," she teased, frustrated that she had her back to them and couldn't see their faces. "Are you even law enforcement officials?"

"Never said we were. Have a problem with that?" The second cowboy leaned close to her ear and pushed her long hair to the side. "My partner says you've broken a law or two lately. Sounds like a punishable offense." He nipped her earlobe.

Charli sucked in a sharp breath, the slight pain on her ear only making her hornier. "What exactly did he tell you?"

Her cowboy from the night before reached around her to tug her tank top hem from her denim shorts. "Only the truth. Nothing but the truth." He kissed the curve of her neck as his hands slipped beneath her shirt, sliding across her skin, inching upward.

The other man found the rivet on her shorts and flipped it free of the hole, sliding the zipper downward. "The truth being that you two had all the fun without me."

A jolt went straight to her pussy. "You know we're out on a well-traveled highway. What if someone comes by? I could scream and you two would go to jail." Her head dropped back, belying her words. If she screamed it would be in rapture, not fear.

"Oh, you'll scream all right." Cowboy Number Two dropped down on his haunches, both hands curling around her ankle. He rose ever upward, rough, calloused fingers skimming across her calf, the back of her knee, the inside of her thigh to the tattered fringe of her cutoffs that barely hid the curve of her butt cheeks. He didn't stop there, his coarse fingers slipping beneath her cutoffs to cup her ass, finding and tugging at the string of her thong panties. "You'll scream when we probe you for hidden secrets."

Her pussy clenched, a wash of juices gushing forth.

The first cowboy maneuvered behind her, flicking the catch on her bra with one hand, the other ready to catch one full, ripe breast as it spilled into his palm. The hand on her back slipped lower and she could feel him fumbling behind her. Then a hard rod poked into her back. "Ever been fucked by two men at once?"

"No," she whispered, her breathing ragged, the assault on her senses, driving her body into a frenzy. She wanted this. She wanted his cock inside her. Wanted his mouth on her pussy, sucking, flicking and tonguing her over the edge of sanity. "Please."

"Please what?" The cowboy with his hand on her butt found her tight, round asshole and poked a finger in. "Fuck you with my finger or with my dick?"

"Both. Now. Please." She tried to turn and face them, to see beneath the black hats.

"Silence!" The man with the deep voice slapped her ass. "Our identity is of no concern to you. To keep you from further discovering the truth, we will have to administer the shroud of darkness."

"Shroud of darkness? You two are killing me." Charli pushed her bound hands against the hood of her SUV. "Uncuff me so that I can touch you. Hell, so that I can touch myself. I can't take much more of this."

Deep Voice leaned close, refusing to let her push away from the hood of the SUV. Before she could protest, a dark bandana was tied around her head, covering her eyes. A thrill of apprehension shivered across her skin. "Hey, this is getting creepy. Let go of me."

"We will, once we've completed our probe." Her cowboy with the deep voice pulled her away from the vehicle and into his arms, tipping her chin upward. "All you have to do is say *stop* and we'll let go. No harm, no foul." His lips brushed across hers, a hint of mint and coffee teasing her senses. "Understood?" he asked, his tongue flicking out to run across her bottom lip.

She nodded, her mouth opening.

He took her, his lips slanting over hers, his tongue pushing past her teeth to tangle and sweep alongside hers, thrusting in and out. When the cowboy lifted his head, Charli tried to follow him.

"Do you want us to stop?" he whispered against her ear.

Her wrists encased in handcuffs and her eyes blindfolded, Charli should have been appalled, scared and angry. Instead she shook her head, excited beyond belief, her body primed and ready for whatever these men had planned. "Please, don't stop."

"Remove her shorts. We need to check everywhere."

A chuckle rose from the man kneeling at her feet. "With pleasure." Big hands gripped the hem of her cutoffs and dragged them down over her thighs, inching lower a little at a time until the cool night air skimmed across her buttocks.

"The panties, too." Deep Voice demanded.

"Yes, sir." As soon as the shorts dropped to her ankles, the other cowboy dug his fingers beneath the elastic of her thong and dragged them down her legs, pulling off both panties and shorts. "I think we have to explore further. Seems there's something of interest in here." He parted her folds and flicked at her clit.

Charli moaned, her body on fire.

"I believe you're right. Let's bring it up into the light so that we can see more clearly what we have to work with," said that deep resonant tone.

Unable to see what was going on, Charli squealed when arms scooped behind her legs and swung her up in the air. She was carried a short distance, then laid out on a blanket, the surface hard beneath her backside, hard metal like the bed of a pickup. "You might warn me next time," she grumbled. Her last word ended on a gasp as a firm mouth closed on her pussy, the hot tongue swirling in her juices. "Oh, my." Her knees opened wider, her hands hooking around the back of his head, urging him closer.

Firm fingers reached out and cupped her breasts. "Better?" The second cowboy breathed against her ear.

"Ummm, yesss." Her words hitched in her throat as tingling turned to electrical jolts speeding through her system. "So much better. But I want to play, too."

"This is serious business. My partner needs to probe the inside of your mouth with his stick."

"What kind of stick?" Charli asked, knowing the answer, her pulse accelerating.

The rustle of clothing and a thunk of boots hitting the pavement was followed by the truck bed giving beneath the weight of another occupant.

Even with her eyes closed, she could tell when the other cowboy straddled her, his knees on either side of her head. When something velvety smooth, yet stiff and hard bumped against her lips, she gasped, her mouth opening.

She raised her bound hands to grasp the rod, guiding a full, engorged cock into her mouth. Even as she sucked the newest stranger's shaft between her lips, her original cowboy pushed her knees wider, his thumb finding and pressing into her anus. A warm wet tongue traveled along the inside of her thigh, teasing a path to her center, that throbbing, needy nubbin of nerves that flared to life like tinder exposed to flame. Her back arched and her heels dug into the blanket, thrusting her closer to that magical tongue flicking, licking and swirling her to the edge of sanity.

Her fingers smoothed down over the cock, finding and kneading the balls at its base. The cowboy above her thrust deep, bumping against the back of her throat. As he pulled out, she clamped down gently, scraping her teeth across his skin.

"Careful, now." He pulled his cock to the edge of her lips. "No biting or we'll have to punish you."

Intrigued by the threat, she nipped the tip of his penis, a guilty smile curling her lips. What more did these two have in store for her? And good Lord, why wasn't she more concerned over being captured by the pair?

A hand reached between them and pinched her nipple hard.

"Ouch!"

"Two can play that game," said the cowboy poised above her.

The little bit of playful pain, and the excitement and danger of getting caught by passersby stoked her embers, bring the fire back into her body, reminding her of how good being naughty could feel. She grabbed for the cock in front of her, lifted her head and sucked it fully into her mouth. Her fingers squeezed the balls, caught between them as the cowboy over her stiffened, thrust one last time and pulled free of her mouth.

Meanwhile, the man between her legs brought her to the big "O" with a few well-placed strokes with that miraculous tongue, catapulting her into ecstasy. She screamed out loud, her voice piercing the still night air, echoing into the darkness. Her body throbbed, her pelvis rocking with her release. But it wasn't enough.

"Inside. I need you inside me. Now!" She wrapped her ankles around his back, urging him upward.

The man whose cock she'd sucked moved away, perching close by.

Deep Voice rose to his knees, draped her legs over his shoulders and drove into her pussy in one hard, swift thrust. He held her hips still, encased to the hilt, his cock pulsing inside her.

Her body stiffened then relaxed. "More. Please. More," she gasped, ready to take this fucking to the next level. She wanted to feel him inside her, scraping her channel in the smooth sensuous rhythm of a lover.

Instead, he pulled free.

"What?" She reached out with bound hands, grasping at air.

Before she could capture his cock and bring it home, he flipped her onto her side. He laid down facing her, his cock nudging against her clit. "I ask you again, have you ever been fucked by two men at once?"

Her heart pounding against her chest, her mind embracing all the possibilities, her eyes straining to see through the black bandana, Charli whispered, "No."

"Do you want to?" the other cowboy asked, a hand caressing her hip.

"Yes!" Charlie lay still, unsure what to do next, wondering if she sounded too eager, too needy. She didn't care as long as they left her satisfied.

With her cowboy facing her, his fingers threading through her hair, she held her breath, waiting for their next move, completely captivated by their wicked intentions.

The other man slipped in behind her, his body spooning her, warming her backside, his dick pressing between her butt cheeks, probing for her anus and finding it. He swirled a finger in her pussy, dragging the thick juices to coat her asshole and his member.

Pulse pounding in her ears, Charli could hardly stand the suspense. Her skin flushed hot and then cold. What would it feel like to have two men inside her at once? Wasn't this every woman's secret fantasy? Would it hurt? Would it be sweet torture? Would they ever get around to it?

She wiggled impatiently against the cowboy behind her, parting her legs to give him better access.

His thick, wet cock pressed against the tight hole, gently pushing in until just the rounded head fit inside.

Charli sucked in a quick breath and held it, the initial pain easing as she relaxed.

Her deep-toned cowboy fingered her pussy, swirling into her, stirring her juices with one, then two and finally three fingers, pushing in, widening her channel. With wet fingers, he found her clit and flicked it, his cock thrusting into her at the same time, bumping against the other cowboy's dick, filling her anus.

Large, calloused hands cupped her breasts from behind while equally dexterous hands held her hips steady from the front.

As her cowboy fucked her pussy, the other man eased deeper into her ass. The blindfold held out the light, but she didn't need to see what was happening to her. All she had to do was feel.

And oh how wonderful it felt. With each thrust, the tension built inside her, the heat of two muscled bodies sandwiching her between them only added to the experience, sending her to the heavens. As she reached nirvana, a burst of stars erupted beneath her eyelids, she cried out, her fingers convulsing in her cowboy's chest hair, the men tensing at the same time as they thrust one last time inside her body.

As the sensations dissipated, the men pulled free and climbed out of the back of the truck.

Charli couldn't move, couldn't begin to speak, every coherent thought chased from her head. She lay on her back, her knees falling to the sides, the cool night air brushing against her ravaged pussy. "Wow."

Gentle hands dressed her, tugging up her shorts over her hips, buttoning and snapping them. Another pair of hands sat her up and fastened her bra, dragging the tank top back down over her breasts. When at last she was fully dressed, arms scooped beneath her legs and she was lifted out of the truck, carried across pavement and placed into her vehicle behind the steering wheel. The clank of metal on metal was followed by the handcuffs slipping from her wrists. Immediately, her car door slammed shut.

As her thoughts congealed into action, Charli grabbed for the bandana over her eyes. Maybe now she'd see who these men were. At last, she'd know the identity of her secret lovers.

She whipped the bandana from her head and stared out the window at the cowboys standing beside her car. Once again, their headlights cast their faces into the shadows. All she could make out were their big grins. Each touched the brim of his black cowboy hat then they spun on their boot heels and walked away.

Charli fumbled with her door, trying to get the window to roll down, remembering too late that the car engine had to be running for the windows to work. Maybe she could follow them to where they lived. Perhaps then she'd discover who they were.

The two trucks backed away, then spun and took off, too far away for her to make out the model or the license plate numbers.

Her hands shaking, Charli reached for the keys in the ignition. They weren't there.

"Damn!" Surely, they wouldn't leave her stranded on the roadside. She spent a precious five minutes looking for the keys, finally finding them on the back floorboard, tucked beneath the floor mat, a note lying beneath them.

With the trucks completely out of sight now, she knew she wouldn't find them. Disappointment warred with a deep sense of satisfaction as well as a need for more as she unfolded the note and read it. The slip of paper contained an address and below it the words, *Backdoor. Midnight. Wear a dress.*

CHAPTER THREE

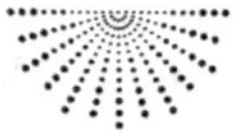

$\mathcal{A}$nother titillating shiver slithered over her body, the body that had been beyond tired while working the bar now pulsed madly in anticipation.

A block away from the judge's place, Charli pulled to a stop in the driveway of a deserted house whose *for sale* sign had long since fallen over. She shifted into park and paused, her fingers curling around the door handle. Should she?

She waited, hoping the phone on the seat beside her would suddenly ring, the sexy-voiced caller egging her on. Then she'd tell him to go jump in the pool himself, she sure as hell wasn't. A minute passed, the clock on the dash blinked to three-fifteen and no ringtone pierced the night.

Somewhere out by Judge Stephen's pool, Mr. Sexy Voice waited.

Would he come out when he saw her? Or would he remain hidden, a peeping Tom, watching to see if she stupidly fell in with his dare. How could a man stay in hiding with a naked woman floating so close? Maybe if she touched herself, he'd come out and take over.

Her pussy creamed as she envisioned the sexy caller, tall, dark and handsome, sliding into the pool with her, naked, his cock jutting forward, the moonlight glancing off his glistening body. The sun-warmed water would caress her skin, lapping at her breasts with the movements he'd create, stirring the surface.

Her breathing coming faster, the heat of the night pressing in, Charli jerked open the door, jumped out and eased it closed to avoid waking the neighbors. Then she ran for the judge's house, stripping her clothes as she moved from bush to bush. If she stopped to think, she'd change her mind. Her stomach quivered with anticipation.

When she arrived at the side of Judge Stephen's house, she hung her clothing over the edge of a bush, perfectly located for a quick escape. With a furtive glance in all directions, she slipped between the bushes and tiptoed toward the pool.

Her body tingled. If Mr. Sexy Voice was out there, he'd be watching.

She straightened her shoulders, letting her breasts jut out. Let him eat his heart out. If he wanted some of this, he'd have to show himself.

Glancing up at the windows overlooking the pool, Charli imagined Judge Stephens restless and unable to sleep, pushing aside the curtains to stare out at the calming waters of his swimming pool. The man was older than her by fifteen years, but he still had a commanding presence, broad shoulders and a physique younger men might envy.

Her heart thundering against her ribcage, Charli made an exaggerated show of dipping her toe into the pool to test the temperature. Warm and soothing, the water felt almost bath-like. She lowered herself down the steps until she could sit on the highest step, her torso above the water, only her bottom submerged, the mound of light brown curls halfway in and halfway out of the water.

Now what? She glanced around, peering into the shadows, trying hard not to squint and give away that she wanted to see who was out there. No amount of scanning the bushes revealed a voyeur, a peeping Tom or even a stray cat. But the skin on the back of her neck tingled, the hairs standing on end. He was there and he was watching.

Charli's nipples puckered, her pussy aching. Damn the man. He'd gotten her so horny, she was ready to fuck a perverted stranger. And he wasn't even coming out to play. Maybe he needed more encouragement. She cupped a hand, filled it with water and dribbled it over her breasts, letting it slide over the tips and back into the pool.

No bushes rustled, nobody emerged from the shadows to claim a ripe, wet breast or any other part of her pulsating body.

Charli's lips pursed and she started to rise when an air mattress floated her way, bumping into her leg. Instead of slipping out of the pool, she scooted her naked ass out on the mattress and laid back, letting the moonlight paint her body a silvery blue. Fully exposed to God and Judge Stephens, she lay back, letting her hair trail into the water, her breasts pointing skyward. Wearing nothing but the moonlight, she floated across the water, the gentle rocking motion lulling her into a surreal sense of otherworldliness.

Still her insides remained tense, ready for more, anxious to reach some level of sexual satisfaction. If her mystery voyeur wasn't going to get her there, she'd have to pleasure herself.

Her hands slid up and over each of her breasts, caressing and pinching until the sharp pain made her nipples pucker and tighten even more. The tingling in her breasts set off a barrage of fireworks erupting lower still, stirring her core to the temperature of a stewing volcano, ready to blast—if given the right attention.

Charli bent her knees, letting them fall to the side of the air mattress, exposing her pussy to the warm night air. A cooling breeze brushed through her mound, stirring more than hairs in the process. Slowly, savoring the feathery soft connection, she let her fingers skim ever downward, over her ribs, past her bellybutton to the curls guarding her folds. She laced her fingers through their softness, locating the sensitive nubbin beneath. Flicking once, she sucked in a sharp breath, her groin tensing and her knees pushing upward.

"Oh, yes," she moaned and flicked again, her clit swelling, throbbing, demanding more. With two fingers extended, she dipped into her channel, swirling in the wash of juices drenching her. A third finger teased her clit, stroking and scraping. Whispering a little louder, she called to the darkness, "You don't know what you're missing."

Her breathing grew more labored, her eyelids dropping low as her hips rocked, water lapping up over her hands, splashing across her breasts. Lord, she felt as if her body would explode. When she did, her orgasm rocked her world, shattering her soul into a thousand shards, sending her spiraling over the edge. "Oh, sweet Jesus!" she called out, her words echoing in the stillness of the night.

Startled by the loudness of her own voice, Charli opened her eyes and shot a glance around. The air mattress had completed a one-eighty, spinning around to face the way she'd come. As she turned full circle, her hand still stroking her cunt, Charli froze.

Poised halfway down the steps, his taut body still fully visible in the moonlight was a tall, dark Texan wearing nothing but a broad-brimmed black cowboy hat pulled low, blocking his facial features so thoroughly, Charli couldn't discern who he was.

Heart beating rapid fire, she gasped and sat up, nearly upending the air mattress.

By the time she righted herself, the mystery cowboy had captured the end of the float, and dragged her close, within sight and reaching distance of the most magnificent cock she'd ever seen. It thrust out, hard, full and larger than she could have dreamed. Her tongue swept across her dry lips and she wondered how it would feel to take him into her mouth and...

"Let go." Charli dragged her gaze away from his dick, her glance darting to the windows above. "If we're caught, we'll both go to jail."

He ignored her, tugging her closer until her body lay within reach of his hands.

Tingling from head to toe and especially at the juncture of her thighs, Charli tried to muster some semblance of modesty, but she couldn't. She wanted him to touch her, wanted him to drive that big, thick dick straight into her dripping cunt.

The shadows beneath his hat hid his face, frustrating her attempt to identify him. "Who are you?" Charli asked.

"The pervert on the phone."

When the man spoke, Charli's insides quivered. That voice, that goddamn, sexy voice turned her inside out and made her body scream for more. "What do you want?" she asked, not out of fear but anticipation.

"I want to lick your pussy."

"Oh." The little word came out on a puff of breath, the last she could get from her lungs as she melted into a puddle of goo, her body like the liquid it floated in.

"Then I'm going to fuck you with my tongue."

"Is that so?" she said, barely able to voice the words, her body on fire, her pussy creaming.

"Then I'll drive into you so hard, you will scream. And if we're lucky, Judge Stephens will watch and forget to call the cops."

"I never scream," Charli whispered, a shiver running over her skin.

A flash of white teeth penetrated the shadows beneath the brim of his hat. "Is that a challenge?"

"No, the truth."

His mouth curved into a wicked smile. "Challenge accepted."

The stranger pulled Charli closer, folding the floating bed until her legs dangled in the water, her pussy lifted up by the doubled mattress beneath her hips.

All she could do was hang on to keep from toppling into the water. Fear was the last thing on her mind, her gaze pinned to the mouth and chin, the only facial features visible beneath the rim of the black cowboy hat.

Clouds skittered across the moon, obscuring even more of his face from her vision.

Then he slipped deeper into the water, shifting her away from the safety of the side of the pool, until his mouth was level with her pussy.

"We shouldn't," Charli said, half-heartedly. She wanted him to take her, wanted him to suck her pussy into his mouth and tongue her silly. But this was all wrong...and dangerous.

If Judge Stephens glanced out the window, he'd have a hissy fit, call every cop in the county and have them locked up for a number of infractions, including indecent exposure, lewd behavior and trespass.

When she should have been hauling her ass out of the water and driving her wet body home, all Charli could do was wait for the stranger to lick her pussy.

With slow, deliberate movements, he dragged her closer, air mattress and all.

He started with a gentle swipe of his warm, wet tongue around her entrance, swirling softly in her juices.

Charli moaned, her hips thrusting upward, urging him to take more.

The cowboy's fingers slid along her inner thighs to her center, parting her folds, laying bare her clitoris. He tongued her, flicking the tender tip over and over until every nerve ending screamed.

Charlie cried out, clutching the air mattress to keep from falling into the water.

Her captor backed up the steps until his dick was within reach of her pussy.

"Oh, please, hurry," she gasped.

"Hurry what?" He nudged her with the tip of his penis, teasing the moist entrance to her vagina. "Hurry and wake the neighbors with your screams?"

"No, don't wake the neighbors." She paddled her hands in the water, trying to scoot closer, desperate for him to slide his cock deep inside her and fuck her brains out. Despite the cooler temperature of the water, her body was on fire, her desire so intense, she feared she might lose it in front of the cowboy. "Hurry and fuck me."

He clucked his tongue. "Such language from a lady. You should be ashamed." He slapped her thigh.

Charli inhaled sharply. "Did you just spank me?"

"I did, and if you continue to be naughty, I might just do it again."

No one had every slapped her while making love. Charli

wasn't certain how to handle this new development. "How dare you!"

"Because I can." He lifted one of her legs and draped it over his shoulder, then he lifted the other, placing it on the opposite shoulder.

Her pulse thundering in her ears, Charli couldn't believe she was lying naked in the judge's pool about to let a man she didn't know do things he shouldn't in a location she shouldn't be. "I must be out of my mind to let a complete stranger fuck me."

Another smack landed on her upraised thigh. "Language, language."

This time, the stinging pain not only made her gasp, but made a flood of liquid rush out of her pussy. "You are no gentleman," she dared to tell him.

"And I count my blessings that you are no lady." He slapped her again and thrust inside her, driving deep, holding her hips to keep her from floating away.

He was every bit as big and thick as he looked, his cock stretching her insides, filling her so incredibly full. He didn't stop until his balls banged against her asshole.

"Satisfied?"

"No, don't stop." Charli forced the words through clenched teeth, unable to gather a deep breath, afraid to move lest he break free and end this exquisite torture.

"You like that?" He pulled back and slammed back into her pussy.

"Yes!"

"I don't think you're quite ready." He pulled all the way out.

Charli cried out and crossed her ankles around his neck. "No!"

The cowboy slapped her bottom. "You'll be ready when I

say you're ready."

"Oh, dear Lord," she whimpered. "Please don't stop now."

He ignored her pleading, his hand cupping her ass, those long, strong fingers, drawing a line down the crease between her butt cheeks to her tight round anus. He thumbed the entrance, poking in gently. He leaned forward and licked her pussy, then swirled his fingers in the juices and traced her asshole. "Ever been fucked in the ass?"

"No." She sucked in a ragged breath.

"Get ready."

"Are you kidding me?" His actions said it all. With care, he rubbed his dick against her anus, pressing in with just the tip.

Charli's breath caught in her throat, her muscles clenching.

"Hurt?"

"Yes. No." Sensations tingled in her labia.

"Want me to stop?"

"No!"

He eased further in.

Tight, oh so tight. Charlie breathed in and let out a long steady breath, the pain easing as the cowboy slid his cock further into her ass.

Holding her hip with one hand to steady her on the mattress, he stroked her clit with the other, thrusting his fingers into her vagina, first one, then two then three. The cowboy's cock in her anus, plus his fingers filling her pussy sent Charlie rocketing toward another cataclysmic orgasm. She held tight to the mattress as her body shook with the intensity of her release. Her ankles clenched behind the stranger's neck, holding him still as she climaxed, hot liquid easing out around his fingers, dripping down to where his cock entered her ass.

When she settled back against the mattress, the cowboy

eased out of her, reached to the side of the pool for the foil packet lying there. He ripped it open with his teeth, sheathed his cock and plunged into her, fucking her until his body stiffened, his cock throbbing inside her.

Her channel clenched around him, moist, hot and full. God, it felt good.

When he at last pulled free, he let her legs drop into the water.

Charli stood on the bottom of the pool, glad for the buoyancy of the water, knowing her knees would shake too much to hold her at this point. "Who are you?"

"Too soon to tell, Charli." The cowboy smiled and touched his fingers to the brim of his Stetson, his face still fully shadowed. "Thank you kindly, ma'am." With that, he climbed the stairs out of the pool and walked away without a backward glance, his muscled back straight, his waist trim, his naked butt too sexy for words.

"Hey," she called out, glancing up at the judge's windows. She would have shouted louder, but a movement at the curtains in an upper window sent her scurrying out of the water and diving for the bush holding her clothing. Dread at being discovered swirled in her stomach.

Charli ran past the houses, clutching her jeans and T-shirt to her chest, not slowing until she found a large forsythia bush to hide behind. There she yanked her T-shirt over her head and shoved her damp legs into her jeans. Running barefooted, she reached her car, jumped in and left the judge's neighborhood before the cops arrived.

Not until she was safely home, showered and in her own bed, did her heartbeat slow and her brain reengage.

Holy shit! She'd just screwed a stranger in Judge Stephen's swimming pool. The dull ache of having been thoroughly fucked in the ass and the tenderness of her cunt reminded her of how good the encounter had felt.

A shiver of excitement filled her, making her pussy cream all over again. Maybe Temptation wasn't quite as dull as she'd originally thought.

For the first time in months, she looked forward to going to work the next night. Perhaps she'd see the cowboy.

Her heart skipped a beat or two as she considered their next meeting. Would he call? Would she recognize him? Would he dare her to play another dirty trick?

CHAPTER FOUR

"Am I being accused of something?" Charli asked.

The cowboy touched the brim of his dark cowboy hat. "No, ma'am. Just routine orders."

That bottomless, soul-melting voice flowed over her like liquid chocolate. The same voice she'd heard on the phone and in the pool the night before.

"We're here to search everyone passing on this road."

Search? The very word brought to mind endless possibilities. "Could you show me some credentials?" Her breath hitched in her chest, her body heating. It was him—her cowboy in the black hat. She peered upward, unable to make out his facial features. Damn. If she could see his identification, she might put a name to this man. "How do I know you are who you say you are?"

He reached into his back pocket, removed his wallet and flipped it open and closed in a flash. "Satisfied?"

"Hardly." She wouldn't be satisfied until she knew who he was and got a little more of what she'd received in the pool the previous night.

"Now, if you'll please step out of the car, my partner and I will get down to business."

Her hand on the door handle, she hesitated, her pulse pounding. "Partner?"

Another man, also wearing a black cowboy hat, stepped up to her door, grabbed the handle and pulled it open. "Yes, ma'am. If you'll step out of the vehicle, we can conduct this search and get you off in no time."

The second man was equally as tall and as broad-shouldered as her cowboy from the night before. A shiver of need whizzed across Charli's skin. Two cowboys? Was she dreaming again? Wasn't it every girl's fantasy to have two hunky cowboys at one time? Or was it only in her perverted mind?

Despite the inner warnings going off in her head, she couldn't stop herself from stepping out of the SUV. As soon as her feet touched the ground, she was yanked into the first cowboy's arms, kissed soundly, then spun away and pushed up against the hood of her vehicle.

Surprise had her reaching out to stop herself from crashing into the metal. Cool handcuffs snapped onto one wrist and then the other before she could protest. With her hands bound together, she tried to push away from the SUV and stand straight. "Hey, what's with the cuffs?"

"Routine, ma'am." Her cowboy leaned over her shoulder, his breath stirring the tendrils of hair over her ear. "Now spread your legs." He braced one of his boots between her feet and kicked her right foot outward.

Forced to spread them, Charli's belly tightened, her pulse racing. "What are you going to do?"

"We have to search you."

"For what?" she asked.

"For a few minutes. Now silence or we'll be forced to perform a strip search."

"Oh, boys, I don't think you know quite what you're doing," she teased, frustrated that she had her back to them and couldn't see their faces. "Are you even law enforcement officials?"

"Never said we were. Have a problem with that?" The second cowboy leaned close to her ear and pushed her long hair to the side. "My partner says you've broken a law or two lately. Sounds like a punishable offense." He nipped her earlobe.

Charli sucked in a sharp breath, the slight pain on her ear only making her hornier. "What exactly did he tell you?"

Her cowboy from the night before reached around her to tug her tank top hem from her denim shorts. "Only the truth. Nothing but the truth." He kissed the curve of her neck as his hands slipped beneath her shirt, sliding across her skin, inching upward.

The other man found the rivet on her shorts and flipped it free of the hole, sliding the zipper downward. "The truth being that you two had all the fun without me."

A jolt went straight to her pussy. "You know we're out on a well-traveled highway. What if someone comes by? I could scream and you two would go to jail." Her head dropped back, belying her words. If she screamed it would be in rapture, not fear.

"Oh, you'll scream all right." Cowboy Number Two dropped down on his haunches, both hands curling around her ankle. He rose ever upward, rough, calloused fingers skimming across her calf, the back of her knee, the inside of her thigh to the tattered fringe of her cutoffs that barely hid the curve of her butt cheeks. He didn't stop there, his coarse fingers slipping beneath her cutoffs to cup her ass, finding and tugging at the string of her thong panties. "You'll scream when we probe you for hidden secrets."

Her pussy clenched, a wash of juices gushing forth.

The first cowboy maneuvered behind her, flicking the catch on her bra with one hand, the other ready to catch one full, ripe breast as it spilled into his palm. The hand on her back slipped lower and she could feel him fumbling behind her. Then a hard rod poked into her back. "Ever been fucked by two men at once?"

"No," she whispered, her breathing ragged, the assault on her senses, driving her body into a frenzy. She wanted this. She wanted his cock inside her. Wanted his mouth on her pussy, sucking, flicking and tonguing her over the edge of sanity. "Please."

"Please what?" The cowboy with his hand on her butt found her tight, round asshole and poked a finger in. "Fuck you with my finger or with my dick?"

"Both. Now. Please." She tried to turn and face them, to see beneath the black hats.

"Silence!" The man with the deep voice slapped her ass. "Our identity is of no concern to you. To keep you from further discovering the truth, we will have to administer the shroud of darkness."

"Shroud of darkness? You two are killing me." Charli pushed her bound hands against the hood of her SUV. "Uncuff me so that I can touch you. Hell, so that I can touch myself. I can't take much more of this."

Deep Voice leaned close, refusing to let her push away from the hood of the SUV. Before she could protest, a dark bandana was tied around her head, covering her eyes. A thrill of apprehension shivered across her skin. "Hey, this is getting creepy. Let go of me."

"We will, once we've completed our probe." Her cowboy

with the deep voice pulled her away from the vehicle and into his arms, tipping her chin upward. "All you have to do is say *stop* and we'll let go. No harm, no foul." His lips brushed across hers, a hint of mint and coffee teasing her senses. "Understood?" he asked, his tongue flicking out to run across her bottom lip.

She nodded, her mouth opening.

He took her, his lips slanting over hers, his tongue pushing past her teeth to tangle and sweep alongside hers, thrusting in and out. When the cowboy lifted his head, Charli tried to follow him.

"Do you want us to stop?" he whispered against her ear.

Her wrists encased in handcuffs and her eyes blindfolded, Charli should have been appalled, scared and angry. Instead she shook her head, excited beyond belief, her body primed and ready for whatever these men had planned. "Please, don't stop."

"Remove her shorts. We need to check everywhere."

A chuckle rose from the man kneeling at her feet. "With pleasure." Big hands gripped the hem of her cutoffs and dragged them down over her thighs, inching lower a little at a time until the cool night air skimmed across her buttocks.

"The panties, too." Deep Voice demanded.

"Yes, sir." As soon as the shorts dropped to her ankles, the other cowboy dug his fingers beneath the elastic of her thong and dragged them down her legs, pulling off both panties and shorts. "I think we have to explore further. Seems there's something of interest in here." He parted her folds and flicked at her clit.

Charli moaned, her body on fire.

"I believe you're right. Let's bring it up into the light so that we can see more clearly what we have to work with," said that deep resonant tone.

Unable to see what was going on, Charli squealed when arms scooped behind her legs and swung her up in the air. She was carried a short distance, then laid out on a blanket, the surface hard beneath her backside, hard metal like the bed of a pickup. "You might warn me next time," she grumbled. Her last word ended on a gasp as a firm mouth closed on her pussy, the hot tongue swirling in her juices. "Oh, my." Her knees opened wider, her hands hooking around the back of his head, urging him closer.

Firm fingers reached out and cupped her breasts. "Better?" The second cowboy breathed against her ear.

"Ummm, yesss." Her words hitched in her throat as tingling turned to electrical jolts speeding through her system. "So much better. But I want to play, too."

"This is serious business. My partner needs to probe the inside of your mouth with his stick."

"What kind of stick?" Charli asked, knowing the answer, her pulse accelerating.

The rustle of clothing and a thunk of boots hitting the pavement was followed by the truck bed giving beneath the weight of another occupant.

Even with her eyes closed, she could tell when the other cowboy straddled her, his knees on either side of her head. When something velvety smooth, yet stiff and hard bumped against her lips, she gasped, her mouth opening.

She raised her bound hands to grasp the rod, guiding a full, engorged cock into her mouth. Even as she sucked the newest stranger's shaft between her lips, her original cowboy pushed her knees wider, his thumb finding and pressing into her anus. A warm wet tongue traveled along the inside of her thigh, teasing a path to her center, that throbbing, needy nubbin of nerves that flared to life like tinder exposed to flame. Her back arched and her heels dug into the blanket, thrusting her closer to that magical tongue flicking, licking and swirling her to the edge of sanity.

Her fingers smoothed down over the cock, finding and kneading the balls at its base. The cowboy above her thrust deep, bumping against the back of her throat. As he pulled out, she clamped down gently, scraping her teeth across his skin.

"Careful, now." He pulled his cock to the edge of her lips. "No biting or we'll have to punish you."

Intrigued by the threat, she nipped the tip of his penis, a guilty smile curling her lips. What more did these two have in store for her? And good Lord, why wasn't she more concerned over being captured by the pair?

A hand reached between them and pinched her nipple hard.

"Ouch!"

"Two can play that game," said the cowboy poised above her.

The little bit of playful pain, and the excitement and danger of getting caught by passersby stoked her embers, bring the fire back into her body, reminding her of how good being naughty could feel. She grabbed for the cock in front of her, lifted her head and sucked it fully into her mouth. Her fingers squeezed the balls, caught between them as the cowboy over her stiffened, thrust one last time and pulled free of her mouth.

Meanwhile, the man between her legs brought her to the big "O" with a few well-placed strokes with that miraculous tongue, catapulting her into ecstasy. She screamed out loud, her voice piercing the still night air, echoing into the darkness. Her body throbbed, her pelvis rocking with her release. But it wasn't enough.

"Inside. I need you inside me. Now!" She wrapped her ankles around his back, urging him upward.

The man whose cock she'd sucked moved away, perching close by.

Deep Voice rose to his knees, draped her legs over his shoulders and drove into her pussy in one hard, swift thrust. He held her hips still, encased to the hilt, his cock pulsing inside her.

Her body stiffened then relaxed. "More. Please. More," she gasped, ready to take this fucking to the next level. She wanted to feel him inside her, scraping her channel in the smooth sensuous rhythm of a lover.

Instead, he pulled free.

"What?" She reached out with bound hands, grasping at air.

Before she could capture his cock and bring it home, he flipped her onto her side. He laid down facing her, his cock nudging against her clit. "I ask you again, have you ever been fucked by two men at once?"

Her heart pounding against her chest, her mind embracing all the possibilities, her eyes straining to see through the black bandana, Charli whispered, "No."

"Do you want to?" the other cowboy asked, a hand caressing her hip.

"Yes!" Charlie lay still, unsure what to do next, wondering if she sounded too eager, too needy. She didn't care as long as they left her satisfied.

With her cowboy facing her, his fingers threading through her hair, she held her breath, waiting for their next move, completely captivated by their wicked intentions.

The other man slipped in behind her, his body spooning her, warming her backside, his dick pressing between her butt cheeks, probing for her anus and finding it. He swirled a finger in her pussy, dragging the thick juices to coat her asshole and his member.

Pulse pounding in her ears, Charli could hardly stand the suspense. Her skin flushed hot and then cold. What would it feel like to have two men inside her at once? Wasn't this every woman's secret fantasy? Would it hurt? Would it be sweet torture? Would they ever get around to it?

She wiggled impatiently against the cowboy behind her, parting her legs to give him better access.

His thick, wet cock pressed against the tight hole, gently pushing in until just the rounded head fit inside.

Charli sucked in a quick breath and held it, the initial pain easing as she relaxed.

Her deep-toned cowboy fingered her pussy, swirling into her, stirring her juices with one, then two and finally three fingers, pushing in, widening her channel. With wet fingers, he found her clit and flicked it, his cock thrusting into her at the same time, bumping against the other cowboy's dick, filling her anus.

Large, calloused hands cupped her breasts from behind while equally dexterous hands held her hips steady from the front.

As her cowboy fucked her pussy, the other man eased deeper into her ass. The blindfold held out the light, but she didn't need to see what was happening to her. All she had to do was feel.

And oh how wonderful it felt. With each thrust, the tension built inside her, the heat of two muscled bodies sandwiching her between them only added to the experience, sending her to the heavens. As she reached nirvana, a burst of stars erupted beneath her eyelids, she cried out, her fingers convulsing in her cowboy's chest hair, the men tensing at the same time as they thrust one last time inside her body.

As the sensations dissipated, the men pulled free and climbed out of the back of the truck.

Charli couldn't move, couldn't begin to speak, every coherent thought chased from her head. She lay on her back, her knees falling to the sides, the cool night air brushing against her ravaged pussy. "Wow."

Gentle hands dressed her, tugging up her shorts over her hips, buttoning and snapping them. Another pair of hands sat her up and fastened her bra, dragging the tank top back down over her breasts. When at last she was fully dressed, arms scooped beneath her legs and she was lifted out of the truck, carried across pavement and placed into her vehicle behind the steering wheel. The clank of metal on metal was followed by the handcuffs slipping from her wrists. Immediately, her car door slammed shut.

As her thoughts congealed into action, Charli grabbed for the bandana over her eyes. Maybe now she'd see who these men were. At last, she'd know the identity of her secret lovers.

She whipped the bandana from her head and stared out the window at the cowboys standing beside her car. Once again, their headlights cast their faces into the shadows. All she could make out were their big grins. Each touched the brim of his black cowboy hat then they spun on their boot heels and walked away.

Charli fumbled with her door, trying to get the window to roll down, remembering too late that the car engine had to be running for the windows to work. Maybe she could follow them to where they lived. Perhaps then she'd discover who they were.

The two trucks backed away, then spun and took off, too

far away for her to make out the model or the license plate numbers.

Her hands shaking, Charli reached for the keys in the ignition. They weren't there.

"Damn!" Surely, they wouldn't leave her stranded on the roadside. She spent a precious five minutes looking for the keys, finally finding them on the back floorboard, tucked beneath the floor mat, a note lying beneath them.

With the trucks completely out of sight now, she knew she wouldn't find them. Disappointment warred with a deep sense of satisfaction as well as a need for more as she unfolded the note and read it. The slip of paper contained an address and below it the words, *Backdoor. Midnight. Wear a dress.*

CHAPTER FIVE

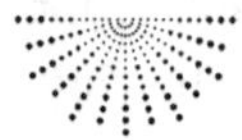

"Are you crazy?" Audrey hissed under her breath.

A smile lifted the corners of Charli Sutton's lips. "Maybe, but I've never been more sexually...stimulated as this." Her hand rose to touch her breast through her tank top with a beer advertisement plastered all over the front. With near-giddy anticipation, she glanced around at the people lounging in lawn chairs outside Ed Judson's new two-story ranch house. If she hadn't RSVP'd a week ago, she'd have skipped Ed's house-warming barbeque to prepare for the night ahead.

"You should have called the cops," her boss and best friend exclaimed.

Charli's brows rose, her eyes widening. "You think a cop would have joined and made it a threesome?" She bit back the laughter bubbling up inside at Audrey's horrified expression.

"No. I'd hope he'd arrest the bastards for gang raping you." Her voice rose with each word.

Kendall Mason glanced in their direction, a worried frown pressing her eyebrows together.

With a reassuring smile, Charli wiggled her fingers at Kendall then dragged Audrey farther away from the group. "Shhh. I was not raped."

"You willingly let two men pretending to be cops cuff you, blindfold you and do carnal things to your body on a public highway?"

Charli cringed at the recounting of the events. "That does sound awful, doesn't it?" But the sensuality of the experience flooded her. She couldn't hold back the smile for long, it burst through, her chest swelling with excitement. "I haven't been this turned-on in months. Hell, years." She flung out her arms and spun in a circle laughing, staggering to a stop, still grinning. "You know the best part?"

"What, that you've completely lost your mind?"

"Yes, no. That we have another," Charli frowned, hesitating before she finished the sentence, "date, tonight."

"Date?" Audrey shook her head. "Is that what you call fucking in a pool and on the highway?"

With a shrug, Charli looked away. "Well, sort of."

"Did you go out to dinner?"

"No."

"Did you have a drink?" Audrey crossed both arms over her chest, a foot tapping the ground.

Charli didn't like the way this conversation was going. Mostly because Audrey had a point. She held her breath, knowing the next question Audrey would ask.

"Did they bother to tell you their names?"

To Audrey that had to be the deal breaker.

To Charli, that had been what made the last two mad, crazy, insane nights so incredible. A shiver ran over her skin. She still didn't know who her cowboys were. Especially her cowboy number one, or as she'd dubbed him...the Original Sin.

"Got you on that one, did I?" Audrey nodded, her mouth drawn into a smug line.

That warm tingly feeling bubbled up in Charli again and she hugged her arms around herself. "Nope. I still don't know his name and right now, I don't care. I like the mystery. That fact makes me crazy with lust."

With a shake of her head, Audrey sighed. "You're hopeless."

"Yeah," Charli agreed without remorse. "I am."

"Well, there's only one thing left to do?"

"There is?"

"Yes, ma'am. I have to go with you on your date."

"I beg your pardon?"

Audrey grinned. "What kind of friend would I be if I didn't protect you from a man determined to take advantage of you?"

"Oh, honey." Charli shook her head. "I want him to take advantage of me. Please, don't do me any favors."

Her friend smiled. "Okay, but I don't like all this secrecy. I wonder what he's hiding beneath his hat."

"Who cares? He makes me smile." Especially when he touched her in all the right places.

"He or they?"

"Mostly him—the Original Sin."

"Catchy nickname." Audrey shot a glance at the group of friends gathered in the yard. "Do you think he might be one of Ed's friends?"

Charli had been wondering that herself. Last night she'd have put money on Connor Mason being her man in the black Stetson. She gazed across at her colleague Kendall Mason sitting on Ed Judson's knee and sighed, wishing she had a guy she cared enough about to sit in his lap in public. Someone she wouldn't be bored with in five minutes.

Her gaze shifted to Kendall's brother stepping out the back door with a tray of raw hamburgers. Tall, light brown hair, blue eyes and ripped. Every muscle outlined by the tight T-shirt stretched over his shoulders. The guy was hot and he made Charli sizzle in all the right places.

Her pussy creamed as she studied Connor. Hell, ever since the first night her guy in the black cowboy hat had dared her to skinny dip in the judge's pool, she'd been studying every man at the Ugly Stick Saloon where she worked, and now here in Kendall's backyard. Her senses were heightened, especially those involving her sex drive. Everywhere she looked, every male could potentially be the one. She was a bitch in heat, sniffing out the dog she'd hook up with.

At the thought of doing it with her Original Sin, doggy style, her nipples tightened and another wash of juices drenched her panties. She glanced down at Connor's crotch, noting how it bulged nicely and wondering what he looked like naked. When she glanced up again, Connor was gazing her way, a smile tugging at his lips.

"Damn!" She shifted, turning away from the gathering, uncomfortably aware of how turned on she was and that Connor had caught her staring at his package. Did she have sex on the brain? Hell, yes. And to think she wouldn't even see her mystery man until midnight. With a glance at her watch, she groaned. Eight o'clock? Really? Four more hours?

"Penny for your thoughts?"

A deep male voice sounded next to her ear. Charli jumped.

Connor stood at her side. Having ditched the burgers, he held an ice-cold bottle of beer, his clear blue eyes twinkling in the sunshine.

Her body on fire, with no extinguisher to douse the

flames, heat rose in Charli's cheeks and she coughed into her fist to disguise its cause. "I don't think you want to know my thoughts."

"That good?" His lips twitched as if he shared her joke.

Did he have any idea what she'd just been thinking? Guilt skittered at the bottom of her stomach. Could he read her like an open book? Probably, since she'd practically been drooling over his crotch.

He tipped the bottle, his throat working as he swallowed the cool liquid.

Charli couldn't help staring at where his full, sensuous lips caressed the rounded edge of the bottle's rim. Her sensitized nipples contracted, her belly clenching.

He tossed the empty bottle into a trash can and turned to Charli. "Still thinking of leaving Temptation?"

Charli's head spun with a dozen questions she wanted to ask. What did he mean? Why was he asking? Was he her Original Sin? Was he testing her to see if she'd had enough of the mystery dates? What if she was wrong?

Before she could push anything remotely intelligent past her lips, he chuckled.

"I take that as a yes."

"No," Charli blurted. "I mean, I haven't even thought of leaving, lately." The realization shocked her. For the past two days, not once had she been bored or thinking about moving back to Austin. All because of one man with a black cowboy hat and a body that completely rocked her socks. She pressed her thighs together. And he had friends!

"That's good. I'd like to get to know you better. What are you doing after the party?"

"Why?" Charli said before she pulled her head out of the sensual clouds induced by her midnight capers and concentrated on the equally alluring Connor. He wanted to get to know her better? What...had she struck the jackpot of men?

He shook his head. "Not the answer I was looking for. Want a cup of coffee or an ice cream cone at the drive through?"

Charli squirmed, she could have kicked herself for her inane response to his first question. Now she'd have to turn him down altogether. Damn it, any other evening she would go out with him, but tonight she had plans. She had to leave enough time to get dolled up. Her mystery man had left her a note to meet him at the back of the furniture store at midnight, wearing a dress, of all things.

Connor's smile disappeared. "Sorry. I thought you might be interested. My bad." He turned to walk away.

Charli reached out and touched his arm. "No, really. I'd love to go out for coffee. Just not tonight. I have...plans."

He faced her again and grinned. "How about tomorrow?"

Her excitement faded. "I have to work."

Connor's brow furrowed. "I forgot...at the Ugly Stick, right?"

"Right."

"That's at night, isn't it? How about lunch?"

Charli laughed. "I can do lunch."

"Great. Then it's a date." Connor stuck out his hand.

Charli took it and shook, all at once awkward and just a little bit disappointed. If Connor was trying to make plans with her for tonight, he obviously wasn't her mystery man. Then again, he was beautiful, Charli hadn't committed to ever-after with the cowboy and the date was just lunch.

"Excuse me, I need to check on the burgers." He hurried toward the grill where flames licked at the edges of the sizzling beef.

Audrey sidled close, her brows rising. "What was all the handshaking about?"

"Nothing." Charli brushed her hand across her thigh.

"Spill, lady, or I'll go ask Connor."

"Fine. I have a lunch date with Connor tomorrow."

Audrey squealed like a teenager. "That's more like it. Then you're not going to meet with the mass murderer at midnight?"

"Of course I am." Charli beamed. "I'm sure to have sex tonight. Whereas I'll probably only get lunch tomorrow."

Audrey slapped a palm against her forehead. "I thought I taught you better."

"Oh, honey, you did." Charli laid a hand on Audrey's arm. "You definitely did. Like you, I know what I want and I'm not waiting for it to find me. I'm going after it." Her core heated and her body hummed with excitement. Bring on the night. Charli Sutton was horny as hell and looking to get fucked thoroughly.

Several hours later, Charli parked her truck a block over at the edge of an apartment building and checked the clock in the dashboard. Five minutes. She'd chosen this parking lot for a reason. After almost getting caught skinny-dipping at the judge's swimming pool, she needed an easy getaway location.

The clandestine meeting had her hands damp and clammy and a bead of sweat running down between her breasts before she even stepped out into the balmy Texas night. Her hair escaped the carefully tucked pins, defying Charli's attempt at a sophisticated chignon. Hell the closest she'd come to an up-do was a ponytail braided and curled around the rubber band. The loose curls she'd worked on for hours had already started falling from the pins.

Damn. Well, it couldn't be helped. If she'd planned this outfit right, the Original Sin wouldn't be looking at her hair, he'd zero in on the V of her long black dress. The gap dropped down almost to her belly button with nothing more than thick swaths of near-sheer fabric covering her breasts. The skirt completely covered her legs when she stood still. With each step, the slits on the sides parted to her hips. If anyone looked closely enough, they'd see she had chosen to go commando as the note had implied. Where a dress and nothing else.

Her nipples puckered as she stepped from the car, her thigh exposed to the hot Texas night. Already her pussy creamed in anticipation of what her cowboy had in mind.

Hugging the shadows, she strode along the sidewalk, the stars above glimmering brightly, lighting her way. As she neared the back of the furniture store, disappointment was quickly followed by uneasiness. Nobody awaited her arrival. The structure looked closed up tight and no light shone over the stoop, welcoming her.

She stopped a few feet short of her destination, feeling silly and ready to run for safety. But the past two nights had been too good to give up without the requisite wait. She shrugged and stepped up to the building's back entrance. No sooner had she started tapping her red stilettos on the concrete than the store's back door opened.

The Original Sin, dressed in a tuxedo, black cowboy boots and hat, held out a hand. "We've been expecting you."

Charli gulped, placed her fingers in his and crossed the threshold. Once inside with the door pulled closed, her mystery man led her through the storage area where furniture was assembled and out onto the showroom floor.

A grand dining table had been set for two, complete with lit candles, full wine glasses and from the looks of the plates, filet mignon. The aroma of succulent steaks wafted toward her, making her tummy rumble. She'd skipped the hamburgers of earlier that evening at Ed Judson's barbeque, too keyed up to eat a thing. Now, all at once, she found herself famished and energized.

She glanced up, hoping to catch a glimpse of his eyes beneath the cowboy hat.

Tonight, instead of relying on shadows, he wore a black swatch of material in the shape of a Zorro mask.

Her heart flipped and butterflies swarmed in her stomach, as she nearly swooned at how closely Original Sin resembled one of her favorite movie heroes of all time. She swallowed hard on the excitement rising up in her throat and focused on the table. She couldn't decide if she wanted to eat steak or cowboy first. "This is very nice."

"Thanks." He smiled. "We tried."

Charli's lips twisted. "That's the second time you've said 'we'. Do you have company, or is there a mouse in your pocket?"

He laughed, the sound deep and titillating, making Charli's decision easy. Eat the cowboy, the steak could wait.

Her Original Sin waved his hand in the air and two more men dressed in tuxedos, matching black hats, boots and masks stepped out of the shadows, grins pulling at their cheeks. Neither said a word, just nodded and pulled out a chair for Original Sin and herself to take a seat.

Charli glanced at them nervously. What was with the clones in tuxedoes? "Are you two going to eat with us?"

"We've already eaten," the one holding her chair said.

She recognized his voice from the previous night.

"We're here to serve," added the new cowboy.

Equally tall, built and yummy, the man had testosterone oozing from every pore. Charli could think of ways he could serve that had nothing to do with food.

He left the room and returned with a fiddle and drew the

bow over the strings in a light, romantic tune, setting the mood for the elaborate dinner.

The Original Sin motioned to her plate. "Please, eat."

While Charli would rather start with the cowboy, she lifted her fork to her mouth with the first bite of an orgasmically delicious filet mignon. "Umm...this is to die for."

"So glad you approve."

She waved at the table, the candles and the food. "Why all this?"

"I wanted to take you out on a date. It had to be private, in luxurious surroundings, with the finest service loyalty can buy." He waved a hand at the two men. While the new guy played the violin, the fake cop from the previous night slid into his role as waiter, adding and removing plates and refilling the wine glasses.

Charli squirmed in her chair, her heart palpitating over The Original Sin's emphasis on the word service. She wanted to question him. Did he mean anything by the word choice? Would the other two guys come into play soon? Her core tightened, longing building with every bite of the delicious meal. Her gaze went to the huge display windows at the front of the building. The candlelight reflected off the glass, giving her a false sense of intimacy. She couldn't see out, but could others see in? "Aren't you afraid someone will notice us through the windows?"

He smiled. "All part of the plan, sweetheart. Nothing makes a situation more intense than a little added danger." Original Sin's brow rose above the mask. "Am I right?"

"You do have permission to use the store, I take it?"

His brows rose, a sexy, bad-boy smile sliding across his face. "As I was saying...nothing makes a situation more intense than a little added danger."

Charli's blood pounded intensely through her veins, stirring up more thoughts than she cared to admit. She gulped an unchewed portion of meat. "Okay, then. Add breaking and entering to trespass and public indecency. I'll have a criminal record longer than my arm before I even know who you are." Charli stared across the table. "Since this is a danger date, shouldn't we share more information about each other? Talk or something?" She lifted her wine glass, sipped and eyed her cowboy over the rim.

"I know where you work, that you are bored with your life in West Texas and that you enjoy hot sex. What more do I need to know?" He lifted his wine glass toward her.

"You know a lot about me...I'd like to be equally as knowledgeable about you." Charli leaned forward, her top loosening, a waft of cool air tickling her nipples. She was almost positive the men at her sides could view her full breasts, should they bother to look. The thought weighted her core with desire.

"You may ask three questions." OS waved his hand. "But be warned. I guarantee no answers."

Charli pouted and asked the most important question, "What's your name?"

He shook his head. "That's the mystery portion of the danger equation. Next question."

Frustration stabbed her chest and she sat back. "Are you a cowboy, or do you just wear the clothes?"

"I've been known to rope, ride, wrangle and build a fence or two."

She straightened. Maybe now they were getting somewhere. The guy was real cowboy. "Are you here with the rodeo?"

He shrugged, noncommittally. "I admit to having spent a day or two there, on occasion."

A frustrated sigh slipped past Charli's lips. That wasn't

much of an answer. "Are you Connor Mason?"

The cowboy smiled. "That's four questions." He waved to the cowboy with the fiddle, who promptly disappeared. The cowboy serving the wine and dinner ducked out as well.

"If you're finished with your meal, perhaps you would care for dessert?"

"I suppose." Charli wanted to know where the other two men had gone and if they were serving more than music and food, but she'd used up her quota of questions.

The man in the black cowboy hat stood and held the chair while Charli rose. His fingers settled on her shoulders, sliding down the length of her arms. The brush of lips at the curve of her neck sent her body into a rush of electric shocks, tingling all the way to her center.

"Is this dessert?" she whispered, her head dipping to one side, allowing him better access to her throat.

"Not quite. I have dessert waiting in another room." His hands slipped beneath the swaths of fabric and cupped her breasts, pulling her against him, the hard ridge of his erection pressing into her back. "Shall we?"

"The table is closer," Charli offered weakly, the rough hands palming her boobs setting her core on fire. She was ready to start the fucking now.

He chuckled, pinched her hardened nipples and slapped her ass. Then he turned her toward another doorway and led her into the room with the bedroom displays, equally exposed to the large display windows at the front of the furniture store. In the middle of the floor stood a king-sized bed, draped in black satin sheets, with red satin pillows scattered across the mattress. White rose petals littered the surface, their aroma adding to the ambiance.

Charli's pulse hammered through her veins. Oh, yeah, baby. This was going to be good.

CHAPTER SIX

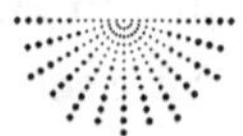

The two cowboys appeared from the shadows, each wearing nothing but black silk boxers, their masks and the cowboy hats.

The cowboy from the night before set a bowl of strawberries and a riding whip on the nightstand and stood with legs braced apart, both hands crossed over a rock-hard erection tenting his silk shorts.

On the other side of the bed, the new cowboy arranged a bowl of whipped cream and a length of rope. He too stood at parade rest, a smile tugging at his lips, his hands cupping the stiffy poking against his boxers.

Charli's breath caught and held in her lungs and she turned to Original Sin. "For me?"

"Dessert has arrived." He smiled and gestured toward the bed. "All you have to decide is how you want it served."

Holy crap! Charli's skin burned, heat rising up her neck into her cheeks. The three men stared in her direction, awaiting her next move. The wide, dark window reflected the soft lighting, the men and herself standing there. Talk about putting a woman on the spot. But wasn't this what fantasies were made of? She turned to OS. How did she voice what she wanted? Would she be embarrassed in the morning, would the men expect more from her when she awoke the next day? Would OS be disappointed if she didn't choose just him?

Holy smokes! They were hot and making her sizzle. Who gave a crap about picture windows and tomorrow?

"I want the works, please." Charli held her breath and waited for his response, praying he wouldn't ask what the works were.

OS tipped his head at the others.

They moved forward in sync—one carrying the rope, the other the riding crop.

With arms crossed over his chest, OS turned to her. "Choose your captive."

"Captive?" she squeaked on a quick inhale.

"You want the works?" he prompted.

Unsure now as to what she was going to get, still willing to try anything, she nodded.

"Choose."

For a long moment, she stared from the man with the whip to the one with the rope. Then with a sigh, she faced OS. "I choose you."

A smile stretched across his lips. "As you wish."

Her pulse raced at the thought of securing this hunk to a mattress and having her wicked way with him. The roles would be switched, she'd be the dom in this scenario. She'd have Zorro as her prisoner!

Taking on the role of his captor, she grabbed the riding crop, squared her shoulders and stood with feet planted wide. "Remove his clothing," she demanded. "Slowly."

OS's two buddies frowned, hesitating to follow her orders.

"I didn't sign up for this," the fiddle player took a step backward. "I don't do guys."

"Now." Charli popped his thigh hard enough to make a sound but not a mark. She jumped at her own brazenness, her body tingling in anticipation of doing it again.

The fiddler yelped and fell in line. "Yes, ma'am." He rounded to the back of OS and slipped the tuxedo jacket over the man's shoulders.

Original Sin's gaze remained locked with Charli's.

His fake cop buddy from the night before loosened the straps on his cumber bun. "You owe me for this."

"I know," OS grumbled between tight lips. "Just do it. You won't regret."

"Oh, yeah." The fake cop threw a smile over his shoulder at Charli. "She's worth it."

OS loosened his own shirt buttons and the fiddler helped him pull it off. "Damn right, she's worth it."

"Enough chatter." Charli smacked the back of Fake-cop's shorts. "Step aside. I'll take it from here." Apparently, these were men's men and didn't much like undressing their buddy. No problem, Charli preferred unveiling OS herself.

The guys moved a few feet away, their hands crossing over their chests like guards in a harem.

Charli gripped the crop between her teeth and reached for OS's belt, swallowing laughter that threatened to bubble up at the bright shiny buckle, probably won in a rodeo. You could put a cowboy in a tuxedo, but he was still a cowboy beneath his cumber bun.

She made quick work of his trousers, pushing him backward until he sat hard on the bed. "Get the boots off," she ordered.

OS kicked off the boots and the pants slid over his ankles.

Wearing only black silk boxers like the other two, he grinned upward. "What's next?"

"Lose them." She touched the riding crop to the shorts. "I want my dessert."

While OS removed his last item of clothing, Charli turned to the other two. "Don't just stand there, lose yours too." Heart pounding, she popped the crop against her open palm and held her breath as all three men stripped naked in front of her.

She'd died and gone to heaven, there was no doubt in her mind.

As they stood in before her, their hands crossed over their massive, muscular chests, cocks standing thick and stiff, Charli almost lost her nerve as the dom. Add the reflection in the window and Charli was surrounded by naked men.

Ah hell, she couldn't back out now. Not when she had so much going for her. She squared her shoulders. "Tie your master's wrists. From here on out, he becomes my slave."

Fake-cop shot a grin at OS. "You heard the lady, tie 'em up!" Fiddler and Fake-cop wrapped the rope around OS's wrists and knotted it like experts.

"Now, you can watch while your buddies pleasure me." Charli took a deep breath, ignoring the dark windows and what might be on the other side. Excitement fluttered in her chest. "Undress me."

Bare feet scurried across the floor as the two men fought to be first at her back.

Fake-cop must have won, because Fiddler rounded to her front. "Hurry up."

Her zipper whizzed down to her butt crack in record time and a hand slid beneath the material to cup her ass. "Soft."

Charli closed her eyes, wondering what OS's reaction was

to another man touching her so intimately while he remained immobile.

Fiddler slipped the fabric over her shoulders and down over her arms, slowly as if savoring the revealing of her breasts. Without the support of her straps, her dress fell to her hips and fluttered down over her thighs.

In an instant, she stood as naked as the men, surrounded by the fluff of fabric at her ankles. She stepped free and faced Original Sin. "See what you'll be missing."

OS's jaw hardened. "Not quite the scenario I had in mind."

"What was that?" She tapped his hip with the crop. "Did I hear dissent in your tone?"

"No, ma'am," he said. He reached for her with his bound hands.

"No, no, no." She slapped away his hands and scooted back to the bed, hiking her ass onto the mattress next to OS. "Fake-cop, over here." She spread her knees wide and motioned for the man to join her.

Fake-cop rushed forward, positioning himself between her thighs, his hands rising to cup her breasts.

Even though the sensation was delicious on her smoldering, lust-filled body, she frowned and tapped his hands. "Not for you. Down on your knees."

The fake cop dropped to the floor and kissed the inside of her thigh, tonguing, licking and nipping his way toward her center.

Her breathing growing ragged, Charli waved for Fiddler. "You. On the bed behind me."

The musician sprang for the mattress, kneeling at her back, his hands circling her to tweak her nipples, his teeth nipping at her neckline.

Charli stared at her reflection in the window. A man

between her legs, another cupping her breasts. If someone walked or drove by now...

A wash of heat swept across her skin, her head fell back and she moaned with the onslaught of tongues and fingers sending shockwaves of need throughout her body. Through the slits of her eyelids, she watched Original Sin as he struggled to loosen the ropes binding his hands.

His blue eyes blazed through the mask, a muscle in the side of jaw flicking with every one of her moans.

She could tell he wasn't used to this end of the torment and enduring it was getting to him.

A smile curved Charli's lips as Fake-cop's tongue touched her clitoris. Sensations tingled though her body. "Stop!" She held up her hand, the abrupt cessation almost more than she could bear.

Both men backed away.

"Whipped cream and strawberries."

Fiddler and Fake-cop leaped to their feet and grabbed the bowls, slinging strawberries and whipped cream across the sheets in their haste.

"You." She motioned to OS. "On the bed, flat on your back."

"Now, you're talkin'." Original Sin lay on the bed, cock pointing to the ceiling, bound hands cupping the back of his head, a smile stretching his lips.

"Fiddler, smear whipped cream on your nipples." Charli waited until Fiddler had the cream on his nipples, then she licked it off, sucking each nipple into her mouth and twirling her tongue around the hard little brown point.

The musician laughed. "That tickles."

"Umm, but it tastes so nice." With slow swipes, she licked the last of the white cream from his chest and backed away.

"Fake-cop, think you can balance a strawberry on that

magnificent cock? Here, let me help you." She grabbed his shaft and held it steady.

"You're damn right I can." He plopped a fresh fruit onto the tip of his dick and grinned.

Charli leaned down and bit into the succulent morsel, the sweet scent filling her nostrils. She chewed and swallowed before wrapping her lips around his cock and sucking it into her mouth.

Original Sin groaned from the bed. "If I cry Uncle, will I get some of the whipped cream and strawberries?"

"Hmm, a distinct possibility." Charli stood and Fake-cop groaned.

"You can't stop now." Fake-cop reached for her.

Charli slapped his hand smartly. "I'm the master," she stated.

"Right, she's the master." Original Sin stared up at the ceiling. "This was not how this was supposed to go down."

"You had other ideas?" Charli slid the riding crop up OS's calf, trailing it slowly across his thigh. Her eyes narrowed as she watched his reaction.

"Yes, but this one's getting better." He hissed as she touched the crop to his balls.

"Fiddler, smear whipped cream on our prisoner's chest."

"Uh, not my type." Fiddler grinned. "But I'd be happy to put some on yours." He scooped a hand full of the creamy confection and advanced.

Charli's pussy clenched, juices dribbling from her entrance at the thought of all that cream slathered on her body and licked off, one tongue stroke at a time. "I'm okay with that." She lifted her chin and arched her back, pushing out her chest.

Fiddler coated her breasts with the white cream while Charli teased his cock with her fingers, stroking his length in full view of OS. Hot rigid flesh lay in her hand but she could only watch OS's reaction.

When Fiddler licked the foam from her nipples, OS thumped his thigh on the bed. "This is fuckin' killin' me." He tried to sit up.

Charli pressed the riding crop to his shoulder. "Stay."

"I'm not a dog."

"Do you like it doggy style?" The words were barely audible as she imagined what that might be like.

He opened his mouth to protest then shut it, a smile forming. "Oh, yeah."

"Then stay until I tell you different." Charli leaned over him, her ass aiming at the fake cop.

When OS reached out to touch her with his bound hands, she raised her crop.

"Not yet."

"Oh, Lord, when?"

Power shot through her at his desperate tone. She smiled down at OS, her breasts dangling over his mouth. "When you're ready."

"I'm ready, all right."

"Not until I say you are." Charli held out her hand. "Cream."

"I'm past that point." Fiddler slapped the bowl in her fingers.

Charli scooped whipped cream and traced a dollop of white around OS's nipples and licked them clean. Her tongue slid over taut muscle, his musky scent familiar and tempting

"Not fair." OS pushed upward, trying to capture one of her breasts in his mouth.

"I'll show you fair." She dug into the whipped cream again and coated his cock. Then she topped it with a strawberry.

"This is as fair as it gets." She glanced behind her at the fiddler. "You are here to serve, are you not?"

"Yes, ma'am." He leaped forward. "Name your pleasure."

Charli spread her legs, and glanced over her shoulder, revealing her brazen reflection in the window, sending her nerves into orbit. God, if she got caught, there'd be no end to the embarrassment. Her pussy creamed at the thought of all four of them rounded up naked and crammed into an official's vehicle. Her wicked mind wondered about fucking all three of them in the back seat of a squad car. "You can lick my pussy, while I suck his dick."

"You got it." The musician dropped to his knees and flicked her clit like he plucked the stings of his violin, gently and with a steady, insistent tempo.

"Umm, that feels so good." She bit into the strawberry on the tip of OS's cock, chewed then swallowed it, taking his dick in her hands and coating it with cream. Charli sank down over him, sucking his length deep to bump against the back of her throat. She settled into the rhythm the fiddler set, rising and falling over her cowboy's staff.

When the tingling began in her toes and spread like wildfire up her legs to her center, she gasped and pulled free of OS's cock. "Stop."

The fiddler stood, patting her bottom. "Best dessert ever."

Charli traced more cream over her pussy and straddled Original Sin's head, a knee on either side, lowering herself down until he could taste the whipped cream pussy she presented. Anticipation tightened her chest.

OS reached for her with his bound hands, looping his arms over her ass to pull her closer.

His tongue lapped at the cream, thrusting through the sweetness to bury inside her channel. He licked away all the sweet confection and stroked his tongue across her swollen nub, reigniting the firestorm of electrical shocks that tingled from the tip of her toes all the way up her body to her taut nipples. Her ass rocked as she gave into the wave of her orgasm.

"I can't take much more of this." With a final surge, OS broke free of the rope around his wrists, tossing the bindings to the side. "It's my turn." He grabbed her hips and flipped her onto her back.

Charli squealed, her heart thundering as the tables turned and her cowboy mounted her, his knees parting hers, his long, hard cock slipping up the inside of her thigh, pressing against her entrance.

"Hey man, don't forget one of these." Fiddler handed him a foil packet.

Charli grabbed for it, ripped it open and slipped it down over OS's magnificent penis.

"Do you mind if my friends watch?" He shot a wicked grin at his partners. "They need lessons in how to please a woman."

"The hell we do." Fiddler crossed his arms over his chest, his mouth forming a thin line.

OS shrugged. "Then keep watch. I think I spotted a police car passing by a minute ago."

"I'll take the front." Fake cop grabbed his shorts and hurried toward the windows.

The fiddler slipped his silk boxers up his legs. "I'll take the rear."

"I'll take my time." OS slid into Charli until his balls bumped against her ass. In one hand, he clutched her wrists, pinning them to the mattress over her head as he moved in and out, filling her with his thick, hot shaft.

"Are you afraid?" he whispered, his breath stirring the hair around her ear.

His question struck a chord inside as Charli wrapped her legs around his waist and tightened, pulling him into her. "Only afraid you'll stop." Was she afraid? Afraid she might fall for a stranger? Afraid to let down her guard and again open her heart?

Hell, yes, she was afraid.

But umm, he felt good inside her. And he'd gone to so much trouble to make her happy and excited, breaking a few laws in the process. Her fingers clenched, aching to touch him, but bound by his hand pinning her to the bed.

Her thoughts swirled into mush as every nerve exploded in her body in a kaleidoscope of lightning bolts all ripping through her senses at once.

Charli cried out as Original Sin slammed into her one more time, his cock sliding deep, piercing her like a silk-edged sword, slicing through what little was left of her resistance and reservations. He released her wrists and she clung to him as he throbbed inside her, his body tense, his face creased in the throes of his orgasm.

"That was so amazing." Charli gasped as she drifted back to Earth. "I swear you made fireworks shoot off, bright blue ones."

The fake cop rushed toward them. "Hey lovers, time to bug out." He tossed Charli's dress and OS's tuxedo toward the bed. "We've got company."

Original Sin pulled free of Charli's channel, a soft smile tweaking the corners of his mouth. "Guess that's our cue."

Charli shot a glance at the huge display windows filled with flashing blue lights. "Oh, my god." A stab of fear raised gooseflesh across her naked skin. She clutched her dress to her chest and rolled out of the bed, running for the back of the store, Original Sin and Fake-cop close behind.

The musician, fully clothed in his tuxedo, held open the

back door. "Duck through the alley and keep to the shadows and you should be all right."

Despite the threat of jail time, Charli didn't want the evening to end. She turned to her mystery cowboy. "Will I see you again?"

He touched a finger to her chin, tipped up her face and kissed her, his tongue sweeping in to tangle with hers. "Guaranteed." Then he turned her, slapped her ass and pushed her through. "Go."

Naked and clutching her dress and stilettos to her chest, Charli hustled through the door, ran barefoot across the back alley and slipped into the bushes. She didn't slow until she'd gotten a block away, where she ducked behind a large Rose of Sharon shrub. After slipping her dress over her shoulders, she peeked out. She could barely see the back of the furniture store. Her tuxedoed and naked lovers had disappeared into the darkness.

A rotund figure poked around the back of the building, shining a flashlight beam into the shadows.

Charli ducked low and waited to make her move until the cop moved on, circling back around the front of the store.

When the danger had passed, Charli made her way to her car and sat behind the steering wheel, a smile permanently fixed to her face. Once again, her Original Sin had managed to keep her interests perked, give her phenomenal sex and send her off in anticipation of more.

With a sigh, she inserted her key in the ignition and set the shift in drive, pulling out onto the street. Only then did it dawn on her that she hadn't gotten a note or message from her cowboy.

Charli slowed for a stoplight and leaned her head on the steering wheel, groaning. She wasn't sure she could take much more of the mystery. Though the sex had been good, the company even better, she wanted to know who he was and if what they had could be more than temporary flings. For the first time in a long time, Charli wanted more from a man than just sex.

As the light changed to green, she straightened, a new determination solidifying. Next time they met, she'd demand to know who he was.

The only other question was, when would her cowboy in the black hat strike again?

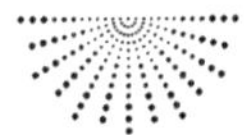

CHAPTER SEVEN

"Three." Charli Sutton handed her boss the dress she'd loaned her. "Count them." She flicked out three fingers, a shiver of excitement slithering across the skin they'd touched, fondled and caressed. "Original Sin, Fake-cop dude, and the new guy, Fiddler. And did I mention, it was a date? A real sit-down dinner and dessert date."

"Oh. My. God!" Audrey Anderson wiped the sleep from her eyes and pulled Charli into her house. "You have got to be kidding me. Tell me everything." She glanced at the clock on the wall. "Is it really three o'clock in the morning?"

"I only have a minute. I need to get home and catch some shut-eye, before my lunch date with Connor Mason."

"Screw sleep, I wanna know what happened." Audrey tugged a bar stool up to the kitchen counter and forced Charli into it. "Speak."

Sliding an elbow onto the counter, Charli sighed. "The night was magical with the three men wearing tuxedos looking so very dashing and debonair, and me in that black gown you loaned me, showing just about everything the good Lord gave me." She hugged Audrey. "By the way, thanks. I don't own anything nearly as sexy and gorgeous."

"Three men?" Eyebrows raised, her friend shook her head. "Three?"

Charli frowned. Maybe that sounded worse than it what it was. "It's okay. The sex was all consensual. Nobody forced me to do anything. In fact, they gave me the whip."

"Sex with all three?" Audrey pressed a hand to her breast and whispered, "You had a whip?"

"Really, Audrey, you're repeating everything I say." Charli chuckled. "Got to play the dominatrix this time, giving out the orders, popping them when they didn't obey." Images from the night floated through her mind, and her lips spread into a grin. "And it was a riding crop, actually, not a whip."

"Like that makes a diff." Audrey's eyes narrowed and she peered behind Charli. "I just want to know who you are and what you did with my friend, Charli?" She crossed both arms over her breasts. "This is so not like you."

"If that's the case, maybe it's just as well." Charli tossed her hand in the air. "The old Charli was bored out of her mind. This new one is having the time of her life."

"Yeah, but how long can this last?" Audrey lifted Charli's hands. "What happens when the dirty tricks stop and you're back to normal?"

Charli jerked her hands free and pushed her hair back off her face. "I don't know, but I'm enjoying it while it lasts. Frankly, when it ends, I might get some sleep. All these late-night trysts are *exhausting*."

"You really need to stop this. All that sex can't be good for you."

"What's not good about it? We use protection, my vagina is getting a good workout, and I'm totally satisfied when it's over."

"Are you?" Audrey hugged her close, squeezing her tight. "I worry about you. This mystery thing can only go on so long before you realize it's not much of a relationship. Don't you want a happily-ever-after with a man who'll tell you his goddamn name?"

Charli pushed away and paced across the room. "I don't know. I'm liking the adventure." Though she would never admit it to Audrey, she had been feeling more and more frustrated at not knowing the identity of this mystery man with whom she'd had three nights worth of fabulous sex. The men he'd brought with him, while sexy, hadn't been the draw. The one she'd dubbed Original Sin held her attention and occupied most of her waking and sleeping thoughts since the dirty tricks had begun.

Coming to a stop in front of Audrey, Charli squared her shoulders and looked her friend straight in the eye. "I'm satisfied...for now. Isn't that all that matters?"

"Uh-huh, see?" Audrey pointed a finger at Charli's chest. "You *are* having doubts, and now you're beginning to wonder whether or not he has something to hide, thus the reason for the masks and mystery."

Mask. Her skin heated and Charli grinned. "He was so sexy in his Zorro mask. I practically came when he said hello."

"God, you're pathetic."

"No, I'm getting some." Her chin jutted forward. "Which is more than I can say for you."

"Point taken. Still, you're having doubts about him. I can tell it in your face."

Charli touched her face. "That's lack of sleep. I am not having doubts. He's very good at providing the necessary entertainment to hold my interest," Charli defended. "The man knows me."

"Does he know you've been hurt before and that you swore you'd never give away your heart to another man?"

Her chest pinched. "No." Charli tucked her hands in the back pockets of her jeans. "It never came up in a conversation."

"Does he realize, a fact I've known for a long time..." With a narrowed gaze, Audrey planted both fists on her hips, "that you claim you don't want a relationship, but deep down, you really want the love of your life?"

Why did Audrey have to bring all this up now? She didn't want to delve into past heartache, she wanted to live for the day. Charli clamped her hands over her ears. "All right already. You can stop now."

Audrey pulled down Charli's hands and smiled sadly. "I was there when you fell to pieces."

"And you were there to pick them up for me." Tears welled in Charli's eyes. "You've always had my back."

"I would be no friend to you now, if I didn't play devil's advocate and point out what's all wrong with this situation."

"I know." Charli struggled to resist the truth of her friend's words. "But isn't it enough that I'm happy?"

"The question is...are you happy enough?"

"Maybe this is as good as my love life gets." Charli stared down at her scuffed brown cowboy boots. "Maybe I wasn't meant to have a happily-ever-after and I should go for a little of that happy-for-now stuff."

"Oh, honey." Audrey hugged Charli and then set her away. "I don't want to pop your bubble. I just don't want you to build a truck load of expectations only to have them dumped like so much garbage when your Original Sin stops coming around."

Charli sniffed, brushing an errant tear from her cheek. She swallowed hard before speaking. "I'll be careful not to get too involved." She didn't admit it to Audrey, but Charli suspected it was already too late. "I have to go now. Connor is picking me up at my place in less than eight hours."

"My point exactly." Audrey smiled. "Connor Mason is a man a girl can count on. You know his name and he's a real gentleman. The kind that picks up his date at her door, not expecting her to do all the work to get there."

Charli swiped at another tear and shook her head. "Keep this up and I'll start calling you Mom." She reached out and squeezed Audrey's hand. "Thanks for being my friend. I'll be careful not to get hurt. I promise, you won't have to pick up the pieces this time."

"Sweetie, I'm always there for you. It just hurts me to see you hurt."

"I know." Charli smiled over the lump in her throat. "Wish me luck with Connor. If I find him nearly as interesting as Original Sin," she shrugged. "Who knows?"

Audrey's eyes widened. "Remember you have to work with his sister Kendall."

"You do take all the fun out of a date." Charli hiked her purse strap up on her shoulder. "I'm off to bed, then lunch with Connor. I'll see you at work tonight."

"Remember, Connor is Kendall's brother and he's freshly back from the war in Afghanistan. Be gentle with the man."

Charli muttered under her breath as she left Audrey's house and headed home for a quick shower and a few hours of sleep before her lunch date with Connor.

AN INCESSANT BUZZING jerked Charli from a wonderful dream where she was Cinderella, being whisked away in a sleek black Corvette by Zorro, his blue eyes flashing, the black mask and cowboy hat hiding his identity.

Charli reached out and smacked her alarm clock, but the ringing didn't stop. Another glance at the green digital letters made her sit up with a shriek.

"Holy crap! Eleven forty-five?" She wrapped the sheet around her naked body and ran for the front door, flinging it open.

Connor Mason stood there, his hand raised to knock, so handsome with the sun shining down on his brown hair, making his green eyes lighter.

Charli's heart flipped several times then settled into a speedy thump. "Connor!"

He smiled, his brows rising on his tanned forehead. "I thought we'd eat first, but have it your way." He reached for her and pulled her into his arms, his lips crashing down over hers.

Taken completely by surprise, Charli gasped, her mouth opening to Connor's tongue.

He swept in claiming her with long tender strokes, the kiss deepening until Charli's knees buckled, her hands releasing the sheet to wind around Connor's neck. Umm, he smelled of denim, leather and hay.

The sides of the sheet slithered down her body, the warm Texas air caressing her backside, along with Connor's rough, firm hands.

For a moment, Charli wondered if perhaps she still slept and this was all part of the erotic dream she'd been in the throes of when the doorbell had rung. Perhaps she'd projected her dirty little trysts onto her more sedate lunch date with Connor, and the resulting dream had taken a spin for the naughty and completely gratifying.

When a horn honked, Charli's eyes blinked open to the bright glaring sun shining through the door where she stood, naked as the day she was born, in the arms of a stranger. Add to it the angry glances of Old Lady Thornton driving by in her 1967 Cadillac. The heat of a Texas scorcher rose up Charli's neck and into her cheeks. She stared up at Connor, her eyes widening.

This was no dream, it was a freakin' nightmare.

He bent to retrieve the corners of the sheet, wrapping them around her, his gaze on her body, not her face. "My apologies. I guess you didn't mean to lose this." He turned and waved a friendly hand at the old woman who had brought her car to a halt in front of Charli's cottage and was in the process of cranking down the window, her face mottled red.

"Have you no decency?" the old lady said before the window was halfway down.

Connor tucked the sheet in at Charli's breasts and hustled her through the door.

"I take it you're not ready."

"I'm sorry, I just woke up." Charli fussed with the sheet, her gaze refusing to meet Connor's. "I don't know what got into me."

"My fault. I caught you by surprise." He kissed the tip of her nose, turned her and slapped her bottom. "Go get ready. I'll just wait here."

Charli ran for her bedroom, nearly tripping over the yards of sheeting before she could get there. Once inside, she slammed the door and leaned against it, her heart pumping like an old-time locomotive all juiced up with steam. What the hell had just happened?

"Do you always greet your dates in a sheet, or should I feel honored?" Connor chuckled from the other side of the door.

"I'm not going to qualify that question with a response." Charli pushed away from the door and scrambled through her dresser for something simple, but not too sexy. After her wanton display of all her assets, she didn't want Connor to think she was that easy.

She paused with her hand in her underwear drawer, hovering over a lace thong and a pair of granny panties. Then again, if his kiss was anything to go by...yum. Charli snatched the thong and slipped it up over her thighs, sliding the string between her butt cheeks. Her belly clenched. God, with all the sex she'd had lately, she should be tired of it by now. Instead, the more she had the more responsive she became to sensations that turned her on.

And that kiss...

She shrugged into a white lacy demi-bra that pushed her breasts up and out, revealing more than the cups covered. Over it, she dragged a thin pink tank top with a low neckline. Shimmying into a pair of worn, frayed cutoffs, she ran a brush through her hair, slapped it up into a loose ponytail and dragged her mascara wand over her lashes, brushed her teeth and called herself ready.

Not a beauty queen and certainly not the sophisticated goddess in the black dress of the previous night, but their date was for lunch, not a fancy dinner. Still, as she walked by her nightstand, she stopped, pulled open the drawer and grabbed a condom from her wishful-thinking stash, shoving it into the back pocket of her jean shorts.

A woman could never be too prepared.

Connor stood by the fireplace mantel fingering a photograph of Charli and Audrey in Cancun, Mexico. "You and Audrey good friends, I take it?"

"The best. We met in Austin and I followed her out here to help get the Ugly Stick going."

He turned to face her, his gaze slipping over her like a

heated glove. "Wow, you manage to look just as sexy with clothes as without."

More heat rose in Charli's cheeks. "I really don't greet all my dates in the nude."

"I'll consider it a compliment then." He held out a hand. "Ready?"

Charli slipped her hand in his. "I guess. Where to?"

He smiled and winked. "It's a surprise." Connor opened the door and waited for Charli to step out.

When she did, she looked around for a car or truck. All she saw was her black Mustang sitting in the driveway. "Are we walking?"

Connor chuckled. "No, ma'am." He hooked her arm and steered her toward her 'stang and around the bed to the other side. A shiny black Harley stood gleaming in the sun.

Charli's heart leaped. "You know, I've actually never ridden on a motorcycle."

His brows rose. "Never?"

"Never. My mother told me she'd spank my bottom no matter how old I was if I ever got on one."

"Hmm. Obviously, your mother never rode on a Harley." He unstrapped a helmet from the back seat and pushed it down over her head, securing the strap beneath. "I'll be very careful. Promise."

"I'm not worried. My mother can't spank me anymore. She died three years ago from ovarian cancer." A pang of sorrow swept over her at the memory of her mother.

Connor's fingers paused beneath her chin and he stared down into her eyes. "I'm sorry. It must have been a terrible loss."

Her chest still tightened at the mention of her mother's death, but Charli forced a shrug. "It was a long time ago. But thanks." She smiled up at him. "How do I look?"

"Good enough to eat." He kissed the tip of her nose and slid his helmet over his head, the dark screen giving his charming good looks a more mysterious and sexy air. He straddled the seat, started the engine and moved forward, making room for her.

Charli slipped her leg over and settled in behind Connor, her naked thighs caressing his blue-jean-clad ass. Her pussy clenched. There she went again, her overly sensitized skin sending electrical bursts across her nervous system.

"Ready?"

Yeah, baby, she was. "Ready."

Connor revved the engine once, then took off, nearly leaving Charli behind.

With a gasp, she grabbed around Connor's waist and held on, pressing her breasts against his back, inhaling the scent of denim, hay and leather—a heady combination on any man, but especially on this one.

The sun warming her back, the wind blowing across her face, Charli closed her eyes and imagined herself flying. The solid muscles beneath her fingertips flexed and stretched as he negotiated the turns in Charli's neighborhood.

When they finally reached the outskirts of town and turned onto the highway, Connor increased the speed, flying along the pavement. Trees, fences and grassland blew by in a blur.

Charli stretched out her arms beside her, and tipped her chin to the breeze, never feeling more wild and free than at that moment.

For several miles, they traveled the lone highway, passing very few vehicles until they came to bend in the road and the turn-off to a tall stone gate with Flying F Ranch written in wrought iron in the archway over the entrance. The cycle geared down.

"Isn't this Grant Fowler's place?" she asked. Charli knew Grant from his visits to the Ugly Stick. He usually hung with Ed Judson, who worked for him as a ranch hand. Grant had built a fortune in the stock market, but had settled on his ranch in Texas, doing much of his own ranch work.

"Yup. Ed introduced me to Grant last week."

"And after an entire week of getting to know each other, he invited you out to his ranch?"

"First day actually. I helped him with a mare foaling. You know the routine—up all night until the filly made her debut. Just like a woman to keep men waiting." He chuckled.

"And she showed up in her birthday suit too, I take it?" Charli smiled, imagining the two men sitting in the hay, holding vigil over the mare. The image warmed her heart in ways she hadn't considered.

Charli was for the most part a city girl, having lived most of her life in or around Austin. But a person couldn't live in Texas without some exposure to cowboys, horses and the country. She had a lot of respect for the men and women who raised livestock, putting in the hard work and long hours necessary to ensure a healthy herd.

Connor rose several notches on her estimation meter. A good man who cared about animals, and wore a sexy pair of blue jeans. Ymmm.

Her legs tightened around his bottom and she inched closer as they drove up the long road to the ranch house and barn.

Pulling up to the barn, Connor set the kickstand in place and turned off the engine. "Grant is out of town and Ed won't be here until later to feed the animals." He spread his hands out to his sides. "So, basically, we have the place to ourselves."

A thrill of anticipation skittered through Charli's insides, her body warming to all sorts of naughty things they could do in the barn, in the hay, against the wood fence, out in the open where no one but the birds, bees and horses would see them. Her core tightened, juices stirring as she slid off the leather seat and stood. She dug her hands into her back pockets, throwing back her shoulders, emphasizing the swell of the pink rib-knit tank top, the patterns of the lace demi-bra pressing through, the thin fabric.

Oh, yeah. Ever since her encounters with Original Sin, Charli couldn't look at any situation without seeing endless possibilities for sex. Wow, what did that make her? A nymphomaniac, whore or a bitch in heat? With a deep breath to steady her galloping libido, she smiled. "Well, we're here, so what's next?"

Connor unstrapped her helmet and set it on the back of the bike. "Another ride."

She tilted her head. "If we're going for another ride, should I leave the helmet on?"

"Not on the bike, we're going to take it a little slower." He brushed a strand of hair behind her ear and grinned. "Don't look so disappointed. I promise, we'll have fun."

Connor disappeared into the barn and emerged seconds later leading two horses, saddled, bridled and dancing around in the dirt, anxious to get going.

Her body tensed and Charli stepped back. "We're riding those?"

Connor laughed out loud. "Yes. Don't look so skeptical. I got the most calm mare of all of Grant's stock. Sassy'll be no problem."

"But there's plenty to do here. Why go farther?"

"Are you afraid of horses?"

"No, of course not," Charli lied. "Only the last time I was on one, I was ten. And that horse was supposed to be the tamest of all of them. I was thrown, ended up with a mild concussion. Had a touch of temporary amnesia along with it."

"Oh." His face fell and his shoulders drooped. "I guess we could drive across country on my motorcycle, to where I had in mind."

Feeling like a downer, when Connor had gone to all the trouble to set up this little production, Charli sucked up her fear and brushed aside his suggestion. "No. I really need to get back up on a horse to get over this fear. Let's do it."

Connor's face beamed. "Good. All you have to do is put your foot in the stirrup and swing your leg over the top." He handed her the reins and climbed up on his horse.

Too proud to admit she didn't know what she was doing, Charli reached her foot high and placed it into the stirrup.

Sassy picked that time to dance to the side.

With her foot in the stirrup and nothing to hold onto, Charli hopped several times then fell back on her butt in the dirt, her pride and her ass suffering greatly. She cringed, waiting for the laughter on Connor's part. What self-respecting woman in Temptation, Texas couldn't ride a horse?

This one. So much for impressing the war veteran.

"Hmm. Maybe we need to rethink." Connor swung out of the saddle, handed the reins to his horse to Charli. "Hold on to Sundance, while I settle Sassy back in her stall."

On one hand, Charli was glad they wouldn't be riding, so she couldn't be too unhappy about babysitting the beast while Connor tended the mare.

On the other hand, Sundance, a large black horse, stood a couple heads taller than Charli staring down his long, sleek nose at her. He sniffed, his nostrils twitching.

"What? You don't like perfume?" She looked away, hoping

the horse didn't try to run off. He had to weigh ten times as much as she did.

Sundance dipped his head and nudged her, sending her stumbling forward.

"Hey. Watch it. You get to go inside next. Just hold your horses." Her choice of words made her grin.

Connor stepped out into the open about that time, took the reins and climbed into the saddle.

Charli waited for him to ride the horse into the barn. Instead he held out his hand.

For a long moment, she stared at it.

"Are you coming?" he asked.

"Up there with you?" she squeaked as realization dawned that he expected her to ride double. She shoved her hands behind her back. "I think I'll stay here. You two can go without me."

"I promise to take good care of you." His eyes shone down at her, a glint of humor twitching at the edges of his sexy lips.

If Charli wanted to find out more about Connor Mason, she had to climb on the darned horse. She held out her hand and placed her foot on top of his in the stirrup. Before she could say a shaky *ready,* she was swinging up and onto the horse behind Connor and the saddle, her butt landing softly on the horse's warm backside.

Sundance sidestepped and whickered.

With a yelp, Charli wrapped her arms around Connor's waist and held on for dear life.

"Hang on, Sundance likes to fly with the wind."

"But—"

Connor barely nudged the giant of a horse and Sundance was off, galloping across the prairie grasses.

Scared out of her mind, Charli clutched Connor so tightly, her face bumped into his back with each of the horse's bounces until she settled into the smooth rhythm of the gallop. Before long, Charli loosened up and dared to look around. Long stretches of pastures flowed by, the wind bending the tall grasses in a gentle sway, lifting her hair from her shoulders, fluttering the strands out behind her.

Like the motorcycle, there was a sense of freedom in the graceful strength of the horse beneath her.

As they approached a dip in the landscape, Connor brought the horse to a trot. Without stirrups to push against, Charli clenched her teeth against the bone-jarring jouncing, until the horse slowed to a walk and finally a halt.

"You first." Connor held out his arm for her to hold onto while she clambered down from Sundance.

Then he swung his leg over the horse and dropped to the ground with a hell of a lot more grace than she had.

Charli's teeth ground together and she almost gave him a piece of her mind, when she caught sight of a bright red and white checkered blanket spread beneath a gnarled oak tree beside a crystal clear stream. The blanket was anchored by a small cooler and a woven picnic basket.

The setting and the trouble he'd taken to pre-plan their lunch date charmed her and she bit back her nasty comment about the wild ride across the ranch on the back of a beast.

"Very nice." Charli waved toward the blanket. "You went all out."

"Only the best for my date." Connor led the horse to nearby shade and tied his reins to the low hanging branches of a willow tree. "I wanted to show you that a cowboy could be a gentleman too."

He moved to the basket, extracted a bottle of wine and a corkscrew. "Would you like a glass?"

"Yes, please."

He popped the cork, briefly spooking the horse and

poured a glass for her and one for him. Then he raised it toward her. "To many more first dates with a beautiful woman."

"This will be our last first date, silly." She frowned as she thought of his words. "Unless you plan on dating many more women."

"Oh, no, I've had my eye on you. You're special enough to warrant many more first dates." He nodded over his wine glass and drank.

Charli sipped more slowly, unsure what to make of Connor. Original Sin had taken a lot of time preparing the dinner date last night. But he hadn't spoken of future dates or future anything.

Connor sat on the blanket and patted the spot beside him. "Sit. I have our lunch all here. I wanted to get away from everything so that we could spend some time getting to know each other."

"What would you like to know?"

He smiled and patted the blanket beside him. "Lots of things."

A flash of guilt swept across Charli's mind. She hoped he didn't ask about her sex life. Last night had been highly satisfying, but she didn't want to lie to Connor from the very beginning.

Immediately on the tail of that thought was the defensive thought of, she didn't owe Connor anything. This was their first date. They didn't even know enough about each other to make any kind of monogamous commitment.

Connor fished out sandwiches, chips and napkins, waiting on her like she was the queen, careful to tend to her every need. "I've always dreamed of owning a place like the Flying F Ranch."

Charli swallowed the bite of sandwich she'd been chewing. "Really, why?"

"I love the animals, the wide-open spaces and the thought of lying naked under the Texas sky with the woman of my dreams."

Her next bite of sandwich lodged in her throat as a molten rush of heat pooled low in Charli's belly. She could imagine the dark night, the stars shining overhead, lying on a blanket much like the one she sat on now. Her lover lying by her side, running his fingers over her cool, naked skin.

Charli swallowed hard and choked on the bread.

Connor leaned forward and patted her back, rubbing his big, coarse hands over the thin tank top.

Her mind already several layers of clothing ahead of him, Charli turned to stare at Connor. "Is that one of your sexual fantasies?"

"No, not necessarily. Ever since I went to war, I had a picture in my mind of what I wanted."

"And what's that?"

"I want what most men want." He smiled and tipped the wine bottle, refilling her glass.

Her hand shook as she recalled what her ex-fiancé had wanted. "Most men want sex with every gorgeous woman they come in contact with."

"Not most." With a shake of his head, he frowned. "Do I detect a bit of cynicism?"

She shrugged and waved a hand in the air between them. "Rightly earned. You know—once burned and all that."

"He must have been a real jerk." Connor traced his finger down her cheek. "I want the house with the white picket fence, a wife to come home to and kids."

Swallowing hard, Charli fell into the sincerity shining

from his eyes. Dang, he was good. She could almost believe him. "Some dream you have there, cowboy."

He brushed his thumb across her full bottom lip. "I expect it will be a reality when I find the right woman."

"Who is the right woman?" Charli asked, her breath catching. "Have you met her yet?"

"I think I have, I'm just not sure she knows she's the right one yet." He poured more wine into his glass and touched the rim of his to hers. "Here's to starry nights."

She sipped from the glass, her gaze meeting his over the rim. "What can you do on a starry night that you can't do on a sunny day?" She challenged him, shaking through some of the heavy content of their conversation.

Charli hadn't thought of houses, picket fences and husbands since her last failed relationship. But Connor made them sound real appealing.

She shook her head. No. She didn't dare dream of that kind of forever relationship. They didn't last.

Right now, she wanted to concentrate on sex without commitment.

Would Connor take her up on her challenge and give her a little taste of his sexual prowess? Maybe demonstrate what he had in the way of competition with Original Sin?

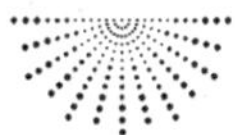

CHAPTER EIGHT

After all of Audrey's haranguing, Charli had looked forward to her time with Connor, hoping he possessed the heat to drag her lusts away from her cowboy in the black hat and all of his friends. A more open and honest sharing of bodily contact and fantasies.

With a long assessing glance, Charli summed up Connor as perfectly capable of turning her on. He had all the right equipment from what she could see. Built like a rock, handsome, charming and attentive. From the sound of it, he was also perfect husband material, wanting a wife, kids and home of his own. Pretty heady stuff for a woman who'd sworn off long-term relationships. Preferring to have sex with whomever, whenever she wanted.

Connor seemed the type who'd want full commitment. Charli wasn't interested in that line of thinking. Not yet. But it would be nice to make love to a man whose name you knew. One you could find in a pinch.

Most importantly, how could she make a decision to give up one hunky man for another without test-driving each?

Now if Connor would just kiss her again, and let nature sway the beast, she'd have something to compare with.

Other than speaking of starry nights lying naked with his woman, he hadn't made a pass at her, hadn't tried to turn lunch into anything more than an occasion to eat and talk. If she wanted more, she'd have to lead the dance in that direction with a little more in-your-face foreplay.

Charli set aside her wine glass and lay back against the blanket, scooting her shirt higher, displaying a lot more midriff. "The wine is making me hot, what about you?"

"Mmmm. Yes, ma'am." He unbuttoned his shirt and slipped it from his shoulders, tossing it over a low-hanging limb. Connor stretched out beside her, lying on his side, staring down into her eyes. "You have beautiful eyes, did you know that? They're a kind of brownish-gold. Darker when you're angry and lighter when you're not."

She studied his pale green eyes, liking the way they appeared almost gray when he looked up toward the sky. "Are you going to kiss me?"

Connor chuckled. "What, no foreplay?"

She curled her hand around his neck and pulled him down to within an inch of her mouth. "Isn't kissing a form of foreplay?" She waited, giving him the opportunity to close the distance. "Besides, foreplay is overrated, don't you agree? Why not skip all that?"

"I don't know." Connor ran a finger along her cheek and across her jaw. "I think foreplay can be even more exciting than sex."

Charli's brows rose. "Are you a man or a woman?"

His chuckle warmed her in places he couldn't possible see, but he could feel if he'd slip his hands inside her shorts. Charli swallowed her frustration and lifted her leg, sliding it along the side of his blue jeans, her pussy rubbing against his thigh. The thought of making love in the daylight had her panting like a dog in heat. She wanted to flip onto all fours and let him slam into her from behind.

Oh, dear. Had the dirty tricks poisoned her from enjoying simple sex with a man?

Connor's lips descended, but instead of claiming hers, he slid them along her cheek bone to her temple, pressing lightly. "A thing of beauty should be savored, slowly and thoroughly."

"What if the thing wants to speed up the process a little?" She shifted her hips.

"Patience, sweetheart. Anticipation is nine-tenths of the fun."

"Screw patience." Charli started to turn her head when Connor's tongue flicked out and tickled the sensitive spot just below her earlobe. "Ummm." A shiver ran over her skin. She settled back against the blanket and tipped her head to the side, giving him free rein with her neck and throat. "That's nice."

"Thought you'd think so." He pressed feather-soft kisses to her neck, trailing them downward to the base of her throat where her pulse pounded a million beats per minute.

Lord, she wanted him to take her now. Forget waiting, forget patience.

Screw me!

His fingers drifted over her collar bone, drawing a line from there to her pointed nipples, poking through the lace of the demi-bra and the thin fabric of her tank top.

Charli's back arched upward. She wanted him to take more, to lean down and suck her breast into his mouth.

But no. His fingers drifted over the swell of one breast and downward to her bare midriff.

Now we're getting somewhere.

She squirmed, his fingers burning against her skin, her body on fire, ready for the ultimate thrust of his cock inside her.

Bring it, baby.

The slow, steady glide of his hand on her skin, slipped lower to the waistband of her cutoffs, where he traced a finger along the edge from hip to hip and sighed.

"Much as I love this, I guess we'd better get going." He pushed to his feet, clamped his straw cowboy hat on his head, and reached a hand down to her.

"Are you kidding?" Charli stared upward, as if he'd completely lost his mind. "We're done here?" She was so far from done, she couldn't think straight.

"Yes, ma'am. I want to get to know you. All of you before we do anything we might regret later."

"The only thing I'm regretting is coming here in the first place," Charli muttered as she stood, pulling her tank top down over her hips.

"What was that?" Connor stood in front of her, his hand sliding up her arm to cup the back of her neck.

She stared up into his mossy green eyes, her breath escaping through pursed lips. "I want to get to know you too."

"Good." He kissed the tip of her nose. "Think we could do this again, soon?"

How about in the next five minutes? "Let me think about it."

His brows dipped. "Okay. You know how to get hold of me."

He packed the picnic supplies into the cooler and folded the blanket, laying it on top.

Charli stared at the portion of the stream where a big rock blocked the water, forming a deep pool, wondering what Connor would do if she stripped naked and jumped in. Would he be shocked? Would he join her?

She glanced at him, hoping he'd have that same thought first.

Instead, the man was gathering Sundance's reins and mounting.

Charli sighed and took the hand he extended, swinging up to land on the horse's back behind Connor, her arms automatically wrapping around his waist.

Well, damn. All that foreplay for what? The most action her pussy was going to get was rubbing against the seam of her cutoffs while riding on the back of his beast of a horse. Charli ground her teeth as her frustration mounted instead of receding, while she fought to contain her rising desires.

By the time they'd gotten back to the barn, put Sundance in his stall with feed and ridden the motorcycle back to her house, Charli was wired.

Like the gentleman he'd been all day, Connor walked her to her door and kissed her on the lips. Not a long drawn-out, tango-with-her-tonsils kiss either. It was a chaste, getting-to-know-you kind of kiss, sweet, but leaving her wanting so much more.

Connor backed away. "Thank you for a beautiful day. Call me when you know what you want."

Oh, she knew what she wanted. What she needed.

Sex with Connor.

Before he could take another step away, Charli grabbed the front of his shirt and hauled him close for a real kiss.

Connor chuckled, his mouth opening wide enough Charli could slip her tongue between his teeth and taste his, sliding along its length.

His hands rested on her hips, pulling her close enough she could feel the solid ridge beneath his fly.

Ah-hah! So he wasn't immune to her.

"Sure you won't stay for dessert?" she asked, memories of dessert the previous night with three hotties in black satin boxers running through her head, fully equipped with strawberries and cream. Crap! Did she have any strawberries and cream in the refrigerator?

Connor nuzzled her neck and set her away. "I have work to do, but thanks for the offer. Maybe after—"

"We get to know each other better. I know." She nodded, not trying to hide her disappointment.

Connor mounted his Harley, his thick thighs hugging the seat like Charli wanted him to hug her.

She practically came, standing there thinking about Connor mounting her.

The cowboy rode away without a backward glance.

Charli entered her house more confused than disappointed. She'd wanted to make love to Connor. So bad she'd almost jumped his bones and raped the poor guy. And all he wanted was to get to know her first.

Nudging at her deep frustration was a softer, gentler emotion, the kind she got when she saw a really romantic event unfolding. The kind that made a person say, *Ahhh, how sweet.*

But where did that fit in Charli's life at this point? She'd had some of the greatest, spontaneous sex with the cowboy in the black hat and his buddies. How could she compare Connor to them without having dipped in his well of sexual talents?

At least, she could mark Connor off the list of suspects. His insistence on being a gentleman ruled him out. Her Original Sin wouldn't give a damn about waiting to get to know her. He'd jump right on and start rutting like a bull on a heifer.

Sexually knotted like a toy wound too tight, Charli couldn't settle in one place. She had to get ready for work, but she didn't want to change or do her hair. She straightened her bathroom, did the laundry and scrubbed toilets to burn excess energy.

Twenty minutes before she was due at the Ugly Stick Saloon, she changed shirts, slipping into a bright red, skin-tight, low-cut blouse that exposed more of her breasts than it covered. Still wearing the cut-offs from earlier, she slipped into a pair of fuck-me red stilettos, knowing she'd regret it after standing in them for four hours, but she needed the added oomph to get her through the night. Her ego was flagging and she needed a little boost. That, and she hadn't gotten word one from her cowboy in the black hat.

Would there be another night of Dirty Tricks?

Ready to leave her house, Charli paused with her hand on the door knob. Did she want another night of dirty tricks? An image of Connor lying on the blanket, smiling in the sunshine flashed across her mind. He wanted it all—house with the picket fence, a wife and kids and lying naked under the stars.

She stomped her stilettoed foot. Then why the hell hadn't he made a move?

At the Ugly Stick Saloon, Charli's mood grew worse. Grumpy, out of sorts and twitchy, she spilled beer, told off a customer and broke an expensive bottle of whiskey before her boss pulled her aside.

Audrey dragged her back to the store room and blocked her escape. "What's wrong with you?"

Charli closed her eyes and rolled her shoulders, but her muscles remained tight. "I don't know. I'm tense."

"I thought you had a date with Connor today. Is that what this is all about?"

"Yes, no. Ah hell, I don't know." She sat on a box of Johnny Walker Red and pulled off her red stilettos.

"Was he a jerk? Did he make a pass at you? Do you want me to take him out? Because I can, you know." Audrey raised her fists and punched at the air.

"No, he wasn't a jerk and he didn't make a pass at me."

Audrey's arms dropped to her sides. "Then why so glum?"

"That's just it, he didn't make a pass." Disappointment pulled at her body. "It was all sweet and no sex."

Her boss's brows rose. "And this is a problem because?"

Charli propped her chin on her fists. "I don't know what I want anymore."

"Let me get this straight—Connor was a gentleman?"

With a wry grin, Charli nodded. "Perfect. That's the problem. I've had this great sex with the Original Sin for the past three nights and along comes Connor, acting all gentlemanly and I have nothing to compare with."

"Oh, honey, your priorities are all messed up." Audrey pulled up a box and sat beside her, draping an arm around her shoulders. "Do you really think all the sexual exploits with mystery cowboy are going to last?"

Charli shrugged. "I guess I hoped so." *A girl can hope.*

"They won't. It's like lust—once it wears off, there has to be something else to keep the two of you together."

"I'm not good at commitment." Charli buried her face in her hands. "I make lousy choices. That's why I swore off long-term relationships."

"Did you really? Or were you waiting for a man worth committing to?" Audrey tipped Charli's up face. "Is Connor that man?"

"I barely know him." She lifted a nonchalant shoulder.

"Does he make you laugh?"

Charli chuckled. "At myself. You should have seen me trying to get up on that horse."

"You? On a horse?" Wide-eyed, Audrey shook her head. "I'd have paid to see that. Question is, does Connor make your heart flip over every time you see him?"

"Yes," Her heart fluttered, even now. "But so does Original Sin."

Audrey frowned. "Okay, consider this...do you know his freakin' name?"

Charli sighed. "Of course, it's Connor Mason. But I *don't* know if we're compatible in the sex department. So far it's only been kissing and foreplay, like we're in high school."

"Give him time to up the ante. Connor just might be the guy for you."

"Yeah, but he's all about commitment, houses, white picket fences and kids." With a deep sigh, Charli leaned against her boss. "I might not be the right woman for him."

"Shush." Audrey patted her arm. "You're perfect and you'd make a great wife and mother."

"I'm not so sure." Charli's eyes widened. "And what do I do with my mystery cowboy in the black hat?"

"You make a clean break. Stop it now."

"I can't do that!" Charli hopped to her bare feet and paced across the floor of the small storeroom. "What if Connor and I aren't right for each other? I'd be giving up a bird in the bush for one maybe in the hand."

Audrey rolled her eyes. "Please, enough with the metaphors. Do you love the mystery cowboy?"

"Maybe, I don't know." Charli pushed her hair back out of her face. "I love what he does to me, the sex-capades he's orchestrated all for my enjoyment."

"Do you love *him*?"

Charli's shoulders sagged. "I don't know him."

"Do you know Connor Mason?"

"I'm getting to know him."

"And do you like what you know so far?" Audrey stood behind Charli and rested her hands on her shoulders. "Is he keeper material?"

That image of Connor standing at her door in the sunlight, grinning, flashed through her mind. His open, honest face so joyful and caring. Blood thrummed in her veins. "Yes."

"Then there you have it. You have to break it off with mystery dude."

"Do I?" Charli didn't want to. She turned and held out her hands. "Can I have one more night of crazy sex before I do that?"

"No. If you want to give this thing with Connor a fighting chance, you have to cut out the others from your life. Connor's a one-woman man."

"He wouldn't understand." Charli nodded. "I'll think about it. There's no guarantee Original Sin will want to do anything tonight anyway."

"And if he calls, what are you going to do?"

"*Think* about it." Charli faced her boss, her shoulders squared, her chin rising. "I've committed to no one. I still have choices."

"You might be limiting them if you make the wrong choice."

"Thanks, Audrey, you aren't making this easier." Charli stepped into her stilettos, cringing at how they cut into her feet. "I'd better get back to work before your customers start leaving."

"Think hard, sweetie. I think Connor could be the one."

"I promise to think on it." Charli went back to work, a little calmer, but no less clear in her mind what she wanted, or what she would do if the mystery cowboy wanted to meet with her after work. Hell, with all the stress, she was almost too tired anyway.

As the clock dragged toward two in the morning, Charli had given up on seeing Connor walk through the doors, his smile warming her insides. Not only that, but she hadn't received a message, text or call from Original Sin. So as far as she knew, there wouldn't be a night of raunchy sex to take the edge off her foreplay with Connor.

Thoroughly dejected, Charli chased the last customers from the bar, stacked chairs, swept and mopped and finally crawled into her 'stang. As she shifted into Drive, she noted a small, folded, brown paper lunch bag caught between her windshield and her wiper. Charli slammed her truck into Park, opened her door and reached around to snag the bag, her heart thumping.

Her hands shook as she unfolded the bag to read the message written in bold black marker on the outside.

"One was fun, Two was great, Three unbelievable, for Four...don't be late. Meet us at the old Jail House Museum. Everything you'll need is in this paper bag."

Charli turned the bag upside down and shook it. A sheer black thong and shiny black pasties fell into her lap. She laughed out loud, her fingers trembling as she scooped up the pasties and panties. "You've got to be joking."

Her cell phone pinged, indicating a text message.

Rummaging in her purse for the device, she jerked it free and read. "No joke. Don't be late."

As a shiver of apprehension slid down her spine, Charli glanced around. Was the mystery cowboy reading her mind, or did he have her car bugged? Either way, the panties and pasties burned in her hand and she struggled with decisions.

On the one hand, she hadn't committed to even seeing

Connor again. She'd told him she'd *think about it.* Then there was this invitation to naughtiness, so tempting, so titillating she creamed just thinking of how she'd look in nothing but a thong and pasties. Oh, did he mean *four* as in four sex partners or the fourth dirty trick?

With the panties and pasties laid in her lap, she shifted her car into drive and eased out onto the highway moving toward the little town of Temptation. She crept along the highway, hoping that the closer she came to the jailhouse, the clearer her mind would be on what to do.

Connor or pasties. Foreplay or sex with her Original Sin.

Still sensitized with desire from her earlier picnic with Connor, Charli almost felt guilty contemplating sex with another man entirely.

"Why? I'm single, free and horny." What more did she need to make a decision? Her foot dropped the accelerator to the floor and shot past a cop doing fifteen miles per hour over the speed limit.

Lights flared in her rearview mirror and a siren wailed.

CHAPTER NINE

Her core so heavy with lust, Charli fought hard against the urge to outrun the law. She didn't want to be late to the jailhouse. The very thought of being pulled over by a cop because she's speeding to the jail house made Charli laugh out loud.

It was in mid giggle the cop arrived at her window. "Ma'am, please step out of the car."

Charli swallowed hard on another fit of giggles, "Only if you frisk me." She bent double laughing, her eyes filling with tears.

"Ma'am, please, step out of your vehicle." To his credit, the cop kept a very straight face.

Suspecting he was one of Mystery Cowboy's buddies, Charli tugged the scoop of her neckline lower, exposing enough boob to make a teenager come. She leaned low as she wiggled her ass across the seat.

The cop's eyes widened and he glanced down at his clip board quickly.

When she straightened, the thong panties dropped to the ground along with the two pasties.

The cop bent to retrieve the panties and lifted them. "Ma'am, you dropped—"

Charli could tell when he realized what he had in his hands. He practically dropped them again.

Before he did, Charli snatched the scrap of silk and lace from his fingers. "Oops. My bad." She bent to retrieve the pasties too. "Can't forget those either." She held up a pastie to her tit. "Although I'm not sure they'll fit."

The cop gulped hard and adjusted his belt. "Ma'am, have you been drinking?"

"Poured plenty, drank not a drop." Charli stuffed the thong and pasties into her back pocket. She hooked her thumbs in the loops of her cutoffs and pressed down, the waistband sliding low, revealing the top of her panty line and a few of the curly hairs over her pussy. If this was all part of the gig, she could play the game.

"I have to ask you to take the sobriety test."

"I haven't been drinking, but if you want me to walk the line, I will." She positioned her go-to-hell red stilettos on the white line and performed a perfect imitation of a tightrope walker. When she spun on her toes to return, her fancy shoes caught on a piece of gravel and she pitched to the side, just barely catching herself before wiping out on the pavement. "Oops. Damned shoes."

"Please miss, I'll have to ask you to come with me." He held out his handcuffs.

"But I'm not drunk. I don't drink when I'm working." She stared at the cuffs, her brows rising, right along with her heart rate. "Oooooh. I get it. You want to handcuff me."

"Yes, ma'am. If you'll hold out your wrists, this won't hurt a bit."

"But I like it to hurt. You should know that." She flipped her hair. "He should have told you."

The cop stared hard at her, his brows dipping. "Ma'am?"

"And you can stop with the ma'am. I know who sent you."

"I don't know what you're talking about."

Charli looked behind him toward the cruiser with the lights flashing brightly. "Where is he? I thought we were supposed to meet at the jail house."

"You can make that call from the station."

"Huh?" She stilled. "Station? What happened to the jail house?"

"We'll see after you take a breathalyzer test."

"A breathalyzer? Boy, you guys really are trying to make it authentic." She grinned. "Lead the way. Have thong and pasties, will cooperate." With a perky sashay of her hips, she marched in front of the cop and slid into the back seat. "Aren't you going to blindfold me this time?"

"No, ma'am. I'm not equipped with blindfolds."

Charli sat in the back seat all the way to Temptation, wondering what the hell? The cop didn't even try to frisk her or pinch her tits. And where was Original Sin?

After forty minutes of trying to reason with the desk sergeant on duty, Charli realized she'd made a big mistake. The cop had really been a cop, the ticket very real and could have been worse than for speeding. Thank goodness, he'd taken her back to her Mustang after she'd been grilled by no less than three uniformed officers, each demanding a look at the thong and pasties.

When she slid into the front seat of her own car, she leaned her forehead on the steering wheel, exhausted, humiliated and pissed. She whipped her vehicle onto the road and drove into Temptation, fully intending to go directly home, do not pass Go, do not stop at the jailhouse.

As soon as she turned onto the street leading past the museum, she sped up, her foot tapping hard on the gas. "You did this to me." Her fingers tightened. "You made me think every man in Temptation is one of your buddies ready to service me. I should give you a piece of my mind." She slammed on her brakes, skidding to a stop in front of the museum. A light shone on the front porch.

Charli got out of her car, slammed the door and marched to the door.

Before she reached it, the old wooden door swung open revealing a dark interior lit only by a single oil lamp.

"Look, I'm not in the mood. I just spent the last forty-five minutes at the police station trying to explain my way out of a prostitution charge." Her hands fisted on her hips. "This isn't funny anymore."

Hands gripped her shoulders and pulled her back against a lean hard body. "Let us make it up to you."

Charli opened her mouth to tell him what he and his buddies could do with making it up to her. Before she could utter a word, a hand slid down over her belly to the rivet on her cutoffs, flipping it open.

All the day's disappointments, humiliations and frustrations disappeared as he dragged down her zipper, his hand slipping inside her panties to cup her sex.

Talk about going right to the source! Her muscles relaxed.

Charli didn't stand a chance of ignoring this man or his magical fingers.

"Better?" he whispered into her ear.

"Getting there."

His fingers parted her folds and slid between, flicking at the center of her desire. "Now?"

She leaned her back head and moaned. "Yesss."

"Do you have your costume?"

In a lust-induced trance, she nodded. "In my back pocket."

"Help her out of her shorts," Original Sin commanded.

Another cowboy emerged from the shadows, wearing a black cowboy hat, jeans and a pair of sunglasses. He knelt in front of her, his hands sliding up her legs to the jagged hem of her cutoffs. He grabbed the fringes and tugged them over her thighs and down past her ankles.

Original Sin pulled her blouse up and over her head, tossing it to a chair in the corner. "Now, pleasure her." Her mystery cowboy continued his assault on her clit while two more men appeared out of nowhere, both wearing the black cowboy hats and sunglasses. Each grabbed a thigh, dropped to their knees and scooped her up, opening her legs wide.

The man in front of her cupped her ass and licked her pussy, his tongue thrusting deep inside.

Suspended on two muscular legs, Charli moaned, her body on fire, her blood pumping hard inside her veins. And she was supposed to break it off...why? Why settle for one man when she could have four, giving her everything her sexual desires could handle?

An image of Connor laughing down at her in the bright sunlight flashed through her consciousness. She pushed it firmly aside as tingles rippled across her body, the start of a mind-blowing orgasm sure to beat all the rest.

"Enough." Original Sin's hand jerked away from her pussy at the crucial moment. The man tongue-fucking her backed away and reached for her cutoffs, removing the thong and pasties from the back pocket. The men holding her thighs, straightened, setting her on her feet.

Charli's legs wobbled. If not for OS still standing behind her, she'd have melted into the floor, a quivering, needy puddle of unfulfilled lust.

"Why'd you stop?" she asked, her breath panting in short gasps.

"We have more in store for you."

"But I was almost there." *Careful, Charli, that sounded like pleading.*

He smiled, his eyes hidden behind the sunglasses. "And you will be again."

"And again," said one of the other cowboys.

"And again," the third repeated.

"And again," so sayeth number four.

A tremor shook Charli's body. Four men. Had she died and gone to heaven? "But I want to come now."

"Patience."

Charli's back stiffened and she swung to face OS, her eyes narrowed. Connor Mason had said the same thing earlier that same day.

The Mystery Cowboy wore the same sunglasses as the others, the lenses reflecting her face like a mirror.

She reached out to rip the glasses from his face, but he caught her arm halfway there.

"Panties," he said, in a firm, even tone.

Charli's ears strained to compare his voice to Connor's. She studied his jaw, his ears, searching for a resemblance, only she'd been too busy thinking about sex to memorize facial features.

A cowboy slowly slipped the panties up over her thighs, his hands testing the firmness of her muscles. He settled the strap between her butt cheeks, his finger digging into her tight anus.

Charli sucked in a quick breath and let it out. "Why dress me if you're going to make love to me again and again?"

"Quiet. You are now our sex slave." He nodded to the two men who'd held her legs. Each had a single pastie in a hand. They peeled the tape off the back and stuck the black-jeweled ornament to each of Charli's nipples. The tightness on her nipples pulled at her core, making her insides hotter.

"What do you mean, sex slave?" she whispered, her breathing less than adequate.

"It has come to our attention that you have been seeing another man. As punishment, you will be confined to a cell, tortured and will be forced to perform lewd and lascivious acts to atone for this infraction."

Her date with Connor? Her chest pinched. "How did you know? Are you spying on me?"

"We have our ways of knowing."

"I didn't come in here to be made a fool of. I came to tell you—"

"Silence!"

A silk scarf appeared out of nowhere and was wrapped around her face, covering her mouth.

Charli tried to protest, but her words came out as a muffled muttering. She was lifted in a fireman's carry, a strong muscleman on either side and moved to the historical jail cell, complete with iron bars, ankle and wrist irons mounted in the limestone walls.

"Oh, you're kidding me," she said into the silk scarf. The words sounded more like, "Oh, mrr, hidd'in mmee." She struggled against the hands beneath her bottom. But she was over powered, unable to fight her way free.

A thrill of fear and anticipation raced through her body as her wrists and ankles were forced into iron, the clamps clanking shut with a finality that made her wince.

The wrist bands were old and rusty. What if they didn't open again. Would she be stuck there forever wearing nothing but a thong and pasties?

That would go over well when families toured through the museum with small children.

With her arms clamped out to her sides and her legs

spread wide, she couldn't go any farther than the chains allowed.

"You will permit each of my men to touch you, taste you and make love to you if that is what they wish."

"I mmm nnnnt," Charli refused, pulling against the restraints.

Original Sin nodded to the first man.

He came forward and flicked the jeweled pasties covering her nipples, then plumped her breasts, weighing each in his hands. His fingers squeezed them like melons, digging in until pain shot to her core, make her gasp and cream. Her arms shot out to capture his hands on her, but the iron bracelets caught her movement. Bending at the knees, he pressed his body against hers, sliding up her torso, his erection pressing through jeans to rub her skin.

"Next." Original Sin gave the next man the go-ahead.

The first guy pinched a nipple, pastie and all, one last time, then backed away, letting guy number two in.

This guy skipped the breasts, his hand curving around her waist, sliding lowered to her hips. He unzipped his jeans, his cock springing free.

Charli's eyes widened. Good Lord, he was hung and her pussy ached for some of that inside her, sliding in and out, her slick channel hugging him tight. She jerked her leg, wanting to wrap her ankles around his waist and sink down over his member.

When her feet wouldn't go higher than his knees, Charli almost cried.

He rubbed his stiff, thick cock over her belly, angling downward to the tiny triangle of fabric over her mons.

Juices oozed out around the edges of the thong. Charli looked over the man's shoulder at Original Sin, her gaze pleading with him.

His eyes narrowed, his own jeans tight around his fly. "Next."

Man number three swept in, shoving number two aside.

A tussle ensued, the men bumping chests in a show of studliness.

Charli didn't care. Their argument gave her a brief respite from torturing her.

Finally, the third man stepped up to her, slid his hand inside her panties and plunged a finger into her cunt, dredging his digit in her come. Then he proceeded to attack her clitoris, stroking it over and over until she panted, her body tense, ready to fly off the edge of the precipice.

"Stop!" Original Sin raised his hand, guy number three backed away allowing OS his turn with the sex slave.

Whimpering now, Charli tried to shift the scarf down off her face with her tongue, but to no avail.

Original Sin cupped the back of her head, shoved the scarf down and claimed her mouth in a hard, thrusting kiss, his hips pressing against hers, the ridge of his cock, rubbing against her naked belly.

"Please, I can't handle anymore. Take me. Please," she said into his mouth.

With two fingers, he pushed the scarf back in place and shook his head. "We're not through." He reached out and unlocked her wrist cuffs. "Suck my cock, sex slave."

She dropped to her knees, all too eager to please him. If she did as he asked, maybe then he'd sink his dick into her and let her have the climax she craved. Charli cupped his balls and wrapped her lips around his member.

He thrust in hard and fast, filling her mouth until his penis bumped into the back of her throat. Grabbing her hair, he pulled hard until tears started in her eyes and her pussy tightened.

His hips flexed, and he thrust again.

One of the other men, dropped down beside her, his hand curving around her ass, tracing the line between her cheeks. He located the tight ring around her anus and slid in his finger. His other hand eased his cock out of his jeans and rubbed it against her thigh.

Charli gasped as OS slid out of her mouth and shoved back in.

The man who'd rubbed his cock against her and whose dick still protruded conspicuously out of his fly, took a position on her other side, and with his fingers, circled her pussy and slipped two deep inside, his cock pressing against her once again. With fingers and cocks in all of her orifices, Charli could only hold on for the ride, her body on fire with need. She wanted to be fucked, hard and fast, praying for a release of the tension building within.

One more man stood beside OS—the odd man out. But not for long. He stripped out of his boots, jeans and hat, then dropped to his back, sunglasses still in place and shimmied beneath her, his head positioned below her pussy, his cock below her chin, standing stiff and proud.

Automatically, Charli lowered her hips, angling her cunt to within reach of his face, eager for his mouth on her pulsing lips.

He took her offering, sucking her clit between his lips, nipping gently on the sensitive nub.

Oh, blessed tongue-action. What more could she ask for?

The torture continued, stroking, pumping, sucking and everything but fucking. When she thought she could stand no more, she rocketed again to the edge of orgasm, her body rigid, teetering. She held it, milking the experience for every exquisite sensation, holding back on her release for a second longer.

Just when she started to lose her grip on her control, OS pulled out of her mouth. "Stop!"

All four men withdrew. The naked cowboy beneath her slid slowly out from under her, his mouth glistening with her juices. Each proceeded to dress and zip themselves decent.

"No!" Charli dropped to her hands and knees, panting, her body on fire, pre-orgasmic tremors shaking her to her core. "Dear God, don't stop now," she wailed.

Original Sin held out his hand and brought her to her feet and into his arms. He kissed her lightly and set her away, steadying her when her knees gave way.

"Perhaps to be continued, sweetheart." Her mystery cowboy's lips curved in sexy smile.

Together, the four men dressed her, their coarse fingers sliding tenderly over her body.

"Perhaps? I don't understand." She shivered, her skin ultra-sensitive to their touch. "Will I see you again?"

"It's your choice, baby." OS touched the tip of his hat. "You must decide what you want."

Oh, she wanted them, all right. Now!

Dressed and still horny as hell, she was led through the front door and escorted to her Mustang.

One by one the men kissed her, leaving OS for last.

He pulled her into his arms and claimed her lips, his tongue delving deep, thrusting like a cock in a cunt.

Charli clung tight, returning the kiss with all the allure she could muster, her leg sliding up the back of his, refusing to let go, suddenly afraid this might be the last time she saw him. "Why did you tease me like that?"

"Four...Play...sweetheart. Pure and simple." He kissed her once more, long and hard. "Just a little taste of what you might be missing. Sweet dreams." And he left with his entourage of sexy cowboys.

Charli climbed in behind the steering wheel of her Mustang and stared as the cowboys disappeared into the darkness.

Holy hell, what was she going to do? He wanted her to make a choice between him and Connor? How, when she barely knew either one?

On the one hand, Connor could be a forever kind of guy —home, family, kids...stability...his name.

But Original Sin? He offered excitement, variety and endless possibilities of dirty tricks. Or did he? Someday, maybe today, he'd walk away without a backward glance and never call her or let her know what happened to him. She didn't know who he was to check on him, to ask him why he didn't come around anymore.

Original Sin was all risk. Was that what Charli wanted?

Her core throbbed and her head spun as she shifted into gear and headed home, with a quick stop at the twenty-four hour convenience store to stock up on batteries.

Enough thinking!

She needed action. Tonight she'd have to initiate her old backup plan with her trusty vibrator. A cold reminder of life before the dirty tricks began...and before Connor Mason came on the scene.

CHAPTER TEN

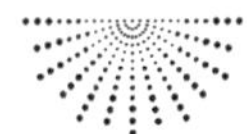

$\mathcal{C}$harli Sutton rushed around the bar, filling drink orders, cleaning tables and suffering the pinches and flirtatious remarks normal for a shift at the Ugly Stick Saloon. Cowboys could get downright rowdy some nights, and tonight was no exception.

She had a lot of thinking to do and working at the Ugly Stick didn't allow much time alone to process everything going on in her life.

After she'd dropped her second bottle of whiskey while filling an order, her boss, Audrey Anderson, yanked her into the storeroom. "Charli, what's wrong with you?"

"I don't know." Charli let out a long sigh and pulled away from Audrey's grip. She walked the length of the storeroom and back. "I'm sorry, I'll pay for the bottles. You can take it out of my paycheck. I just can't concentrate on work."

Audrey shook her head. "Forget the whiskey. Maybe you should take the night off."

"No!" Charli stilled and her hands drew into fists. She couldn't leave. Connor Mason might show up. To make the decisions she needed to make, she wanted all the time she could get with the man. "I really need to work."

"Honey, you look exhausted. Between dating Connor during the day and your after-hours rendezvous with your crew of bad boys, I'd say you're burning the candle at both ends. If you're not careful, your butt's gonna get burned. Are you getting *any* sleep?"

Unable to keep up the façade, Charli's shoulders dipped and her throat thickened. "No." She sat on a stack of boxes full of liquor. "Even when I do have time to sleep, I can't stop thinking. Five days have passed since the last time I saw either Connor or my so-called bad boys. I don't know what I did wrong." She buried her face in her hands, despair dragging her down.

Audrey's brows rose into the strawberry-blond hair hang down over her forehead. "Aren't you the girl who was complaining there wasn't anything to do in Temptation, Texas?"

With a snort, Charli looked up. "Yeah. A million years ago."

"Darlin', that was only nine days ago." Audrey propped a hand on one hip. "Didn't you discover plenty was happenin' in this little corner of our world?"

"Sure, as long as I had company." Charli waved her hands wide, staring around at the boxes of supplies. "Now, nothing. I'm back to square one. Connor hasn't been by in five days, I haven't gotten a note, text, call, or fly-by from my mystery cowboy or even one of his crew of hotties."

"Does Connor know about your mystery meetings? Did you tell him?" Audrey asked.

"Are you kidding? He's an all-or-nothing kinda guy." Charli jumped up and paced to the end of the room and back again. "If I told him anything, he'd be out of my life faster than I could say, *See ya*." She tipped an imaginary cowboy hat and sighed.

"Do you want to be with Connor?"

"I don't know," Charli wailed, warmth flowing throughout her body. "I've only been on one date with the man, talked to him once in the bar and once at Ed's house. I've kissed him three times. What's to know?" Except those kisses had been...well...hot.

"And Mystery Cowboy...no wait...you were calling him Original Sin...Hmm..." Audrey tapped a manicured nail to her chin. "No news on who he is?"

"None." Charli's heart ached. What had she done to piss off all the men in her life? "And no way of contacting him."

Audrey's eyes narrowed. "He called you on your cell phone. Did his number show up on your caller id?"

"Blocked Sender." Charli leaned her forehead against a shelf. "I'm so screwed." The irony hit and she raised her head. "Strike that, I'm so *not* screwed. Four nights of unprecedented sex, then nothing for five days. One date with a man who wants to get to know me before we have sex , then he doesn't ask me out again." Charli banged her forehead against the shelf, hoping the pain would help her to focus on what was important. No luck.

"What is it you want out of a relationship?" Audrey asked.

Charli straightened. "Sex!"

"And?"

"More sex!" Charli spun in a circle, her arms splaying out, hitting the boxes stacked on the shelves. She came to a stop, grimacing, knowing what her friend was going to say before she even opened her mouth. Yeah, it was time for the truth to be revealed.

Audrey's lips twisted and she asked exactly what Charli expected, "And after you've had sex?"

Charli stared into a corner, without really seeing the broom and mop hanging there. "Someone to talk to. A man who'll stick around long enough that I can get to know him." She glanced at Audrey. "Am I asking too much?"

"No, honey, you're not." Audrey pulled her into hug, her hands stroking the back of Charli's head.

Sinking into the warmth of Audrey's body, Charli didn't want to move, didn't want to come out and face reality. But she had to. She needed to get back to work. "I feel so crappy," Charli said into Audrey's shoulder. "What do I do?"

Audrey sighed. "You are in a pickle, aren't you, sweetie?"

"I've burned up a brand new set of batteries in my vibrator." Charli pushed away from her friend's warmth, her gaze dropping to her own boots. She almost wished the floor would open up and swallow her, so that she didn't have to face a room full of men, none of which she gave a damn about. "I can't live this way."

Grabbing her arms, Audrey turned Charli to face her. "Baby girl, it's time you turned the tables on those men."

"What do you mean?"

Audrey balled a fist and punched the air. "Fight fire with fire."

Charli stared wide-eyed at Audrey, trying to make sense of what her boss was telling her. Finally, she threw her hands in the air. "I don't have a clue what you're talking about."

"If you want those men to make a move, you need to make one of your own."

Make a move? Her shoulders sagging, Charli moaned. "I have no way of getting hold of Original Sin. He shows up when he wants and doesn't leave a calling card."

"Then screw him." Audrey frowned. "Go for the bird in hand. You know where to find Connor."

"Connor Mason?" A deep male voice boomed into the

tiny storeroom as Jackson Gray Wolf, Audrey's Kiowa cowboy boyfriend stepped inside.

Greta Sue hovered behind him in the doorway. "Found him lurking," she said. "I can throw him out, if you want." The bouncer flexed her shoulders, giving no doubt she could take on a grown man.

"You better vouch for me. Greta Sue would win if I tried to take her on." Jackson grinned. "She knows I won't hit a girl."

Greta Sue frowned, her fisted hands landing on her hips. "I'm not a girl."

Jackson stepped up to the big woman and bestowed one of his most knee-melting smiles. Then he leaned close to her ear, whispering softly, but loud enough Charli could hear what he said, "I'll bet beneath that kick-ass exterior, you're just a softy inside, waiting for the right man...the right kiss..."

The woman's face bloomed red and she scooted back really fast. "Keep it up, Gray Wolf, and I'll eat your balls as oyster shooters."

"Uh-huh." Jackson winked. "That's what I thought."

"Eh-hem. Jackson, honey." Audrey crossed both arms over her chest. "Quit flirting with Greta Sue. I'm getting jealous."

Jackson spun and grabbed Audrey in a bone-crunching bear hug, kissing her soundly before he set her on her feet. "Better?"

Audrey frowned, though her lips quirked at the corners.

Charli's chest tightened at the way Audrey's eyes shone with her love for Jackson. Why couldn't she find someone she could be that crazy about? Hell, she might have, if she could just get more time with him...them...whoever! "I'm dying here. It's been five days since I got so much as a hug."

"We can make it a threesome." Jackson opened his arms, inviting Charli into his embrace.

Audrey slapped his chest. "Your threesome days are over, buddy. Either help us or scoot."

Jackson kissed the tip of Audrey's nose. "I love it when you tell me what to do. Especially when you're naked."

Charli's gut tightened as an image of a naked Audrey and Jackson flashed through her mind, making her own body warm, her pussy aching for a little action. She crossed her legs, willing the desire to abate, for now. "Not helping."

"Jackson..." Audrey's face flamed. "Charli needs to seduce Connor. Any suggestions on how to go about it?"

The Kiowa cowboy's eyes widened as he shifted his attention from Audrey to Charli. "You need to know how to seduce Connor?" He gaze switched back to Audrey and the skin around his eyes tightened. "Is this a trick question?"

Charli flung up her hands. "You see? Jackson thinks it's stupid. What am I supposed to do?"

Stepping backward, Jackson held up his hands in surrender. "I don't think it's stupid to seduce Connor. I just would think it was obvious how to go about it."

"Honey." Audrey circled an arm around Jackson, "if the how was so obvious, we wouldn't be asking."

Slipping an arm over Audrey's and Charli's shoulders, Jackson grinned. "Men are simple creatures. Don't make it hard." His hand slid downward on Audrey's back, cupping her ass. "Well, maybe a little hard. Those parts that are supposed to be, anyway."

With a wiggle, she shoved away his hand. "Give us a clue as to what you're talking about, please."

"Seriously?" Jackson stood wide-eyed. "The five-second sure-fire way to seduce a man is to get naked in front of him."

Charli raised her face to the ceiling. "I can't march up to

his house naked. The seduction has to be more subtle than that."

Jackson's brow wrinkled. "Why do you want to seduce him?"

As she stared across Jackson's chest at Audrey, Charli's face burned. "Does he know?"

"No." Audrey shook her head. "Do you want him to know?"

Charli's forehead scrunched. "Yeah, sure. Why not? I'm not getting any lately anyway."

"Are you two talking in code or something?" Jackson let go of the women and crossed his arms. "What part about 'men are simple' did you not understand?"

Audrey hooked his arm and led him to a stack of boxes, where she seated him. "It's like this..." She gathered a deep breath and launched. "Charli was thinkin' of leavin'."

Jackson's head jerked toward Charli. "The Ugly Stick or Temptation altogether?"

Charli moaned. "This will take too long."

Audrey shot a frown at Charli, and pressed a finger to Jackson's lips. "Don't interrupt until I finish, please. As I was saying, Charli was going to leave Temptation, on account of she was bored. Until a mystery man tempted her to skinny dip in Judge Stephen's pool."

Jackson grinned and his mouth opened, but before he could say anything, Audrey continued. "She took him up on the dare, skinny-dipped and did it with this man."

"Who is he?" Jackson slipped in the question while Audrey took a breath.

"She doesn't know. He wore a black cowboy hat pulled down low." Audrey waved a hand. "Anyway, the next night he pulled her over on the highway with a buddy of his and the three of them did it in the back of a pickup."

Jackson shifted on the boxes, leaning toward Audrey. "You're turning me on."

Audrey grinned. "I know, it does, doesn't it?"

"Audrey..." Charli waved her hands in her boss's face. "I need to get back to work sometime."

"So the next night she's meets her mystery man at the furniture store where he treats her to dinner and desert with two other guys."

"Charli and three men?" Jackson choked back a laugh, his eyes getting rounder. "Our sweet, staid, bartender Charli?"

Charli winced at the 'staid' part.

Audrey nodded. "It gets kinkier."

Jackson's brows dipped. "And I take it she still doesn't know who this mystery cowboy or any of his buddies are?" He shot a narrow-eyed glance at Charli.

"Nope." Audrey added her frown to Jackson's. "That has me worried too."

Maybe telling Jackson wasn't such a good idea. Charli's face burned and her body heated.

Audrey continued, "The next day she had a date with Connor Mason."

"Ah..." Jackson raised a finger. "Is he the mystery cowboy?"

Charli shrugged. "I doubt it. He took me out on his ranch, we had a picnic and he never made a single move on me."

Jackson's brow wrinkled. "Did you get naked?"

"No."

The Kiowa cowboy raised his hands palms upward. "I told you, men are simple. Get naked."

"Good grief. We're wasting our time." Charli stood to leave.

"Wait. I'm not done filling him in. You might want to stay to make sure I get it right." Audrey turned her attention back to Jackson. "That night, she had another meeting with her mystery cowboy at the historical jail house, complete with manacles and kinky sex with four men this time."

Jackson whistled. "I'm jealous."

"Yeah, you and me both." Audrey stepped back. "And that's it."

"What do you mean?" Jackson stood.

"Nothing for the past five days." Charli paced across the space in front of Jackson and Audrey. "No phone calls, no dates, no sex."

"Did you call them?" Audrey's cowboy asked.

Charli sighed, wishing she'd had the mental wherewithal to ask Original Sin for his number. "I don't have the mystery cowboy's number, or name, for that matter." How was she supposed to remember anything when she'd been treated to orgasmic sex with multiple partners tending to her every need and fantasy? Sheesh, she'd struggled just to catch her breath.

"What about Connor?" Audrey asked.

"I must not have impressed him on our first date." Charli tipped back her head and squeezed shut her eyes. "He hasn't arranged for another."

"Then call him." Audrey slipped an arm around Charli's waist and squeezed. "Maybe he's shy."

Jackson shoved his thumbs into his belt loops. "Why not just go up to him and ask him out?"

"I haven't run into him in five days." Charli's frustration bubbled over. "What do you expect me to do, drive over to his place and knock on his door?"

A frown pulled Jackson's brows together. "No. Ask him here. He's in the saloon."

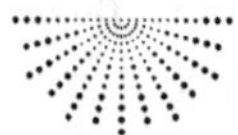

CHAPTER ELEVEN

Charli's heart skipped several beats and her lungs refused to work.

Audrey's eyes brightened. "See? He came in to see you." She shoved Charli toward the door. "Ask him out, then get naked like Jackson said."

"I can't just ask him out." Charli spun from the door and retreated back into the storeroom, face burning, and her palms sweating. "I need a plan. Good God, help me with a plan."

Bless the Kiowa Cowboy for the big dumb lug he was. He slipped his hand around Charli's waist and hugged her. "It's okay. I got one for you."

Audrey and Charli both looked up and spoke at the same time. "You do?"

"Yeah. Call it...I don't know...How about Five Steps to Seduction?" He grinned.

Charli's heart slipped into her gut like a ball of lead. "You're not helping with funny titles. I need a real, concrete plan."

Jackson's hand tightened on her waist. "I'm getting there.

Keep your pants on."

"They're on...that's the problem," Charli wailed.

"Step one," Jackson continued. "It's all like hunting. First you got to get the right equipment." He pushed Charli out in front of him and reached toward her breasts, his hands stopping before he touched. "May I?"

Charli glared, resisting the urge to step back. What the hell was he up to? "I have the right equipment, if he's into women." She pushed up her boobs, letting them fall back in place with a perky bounce.

Audrey 's lips twisted and her eyes narrowed. "I see where you're going." She grabbed Charli's shirt and dragged it up her torso. "Take it off."

Charli gasped and knocked away Audrey's hands. "What are you doing?"

"Take off your bra, honey, it's not doing a thing for you." Audrey whipped her own T-shirt over her head and unclasped her bra, sliding the straps down over her shoulders. "Here, use mine. It's guaranteed to lift and push the girls together, giving you some hot cleavage."

Jackson's smile stretched across his face and he reached for Audrey's breasts. "What a friend." He cupped one, bending to take a nipple into his mouth.

Just watching Jackson play with Audrey's breasts brought back too many images of Original Sin doing the same to her own. Her nipples tightened into buds, and Charli creamed in her panties.

Audrey popped the top of his head. "Later, Casanova. We need to focus on Charli." She held her bra out by the strap, while wiggling the fingers of her other hand. "Give me yours. I don't want to start a riot in the bar by going braless."

"You'd have every horndog in the county drooling, babe." Jackson pulled Audrey's backside against the ridge rising in his pants. "Including me." His hands cupped her breasts like Audrey's own, personal bra.

"Cut it out, you two. You're making me horny for some girl love." Charli pulled her arms inside her T-shirt and unhooked her bra beneath the fabric, wiggling out of it. "I don't know. You look bigger than me."

"Only because the bra, dear. Trust me. It's amazing." Audrey snuggled against Jackson, a hand slipping between their bodies, caressing his denim-clad crotch.

Five days since she'd had sex and Charli was forced to watch Audrey and Jackson nearly having an orgasm in front of her. The logistics of putting Audrey's bra on under her T-shirt, plus the frustration of the two getting some while she wasn't made anger replace desire. Charli ripped her shirt up over her head and flung it on a box, grabbed Audrey's bra, hooked it around her waist and pulled the straps up.

Jackson whistled. "Nice breasts. Now, see? That's all it took. She gets a little naked, I get a lot horny."

Audrey slapped him, playfully. "Keep it in your pants until we're alone, will you?"

Jackson looked all innocent. "Just saying."

With a glance downward, Charli had to admit the bra pushed her up, with just enough coverage the cups barely hid her nipples, and displayed a whole lot of cleavage. Anxious to get outside, she grabbed her T-shirt and pulled it over her head.

"Are you trying to attract a man or a lesbian?" Jackson asked with a wave of his hand at her body. "Either way, you're missing the point."

"Oh, no, no, no. Jackson's right." Audrey yanked the shirt back over Charli's head and tossed it behind a stack of boxes. "Covers far too much." She marched to the rack of costumes the male dancers used on Ladies' Night Out at the saloon and selected a cowboy vest that had only one snap at the center. She slipped the vest over Charli's arms and pulled the lapels together in the front, securing the snap on level with Charli's bellybutton.

Charli glanced down at her exposed chest and sucked in a breath. "You're kidding, right?"

Audrey stood back and tapped a finger on her chin. "Still needs something."

"I can't go out there like this." Charli tugged up the vest, in an attempt to cover more of her boobs.

"Why not?"Audrey pulled Charli's hands down to her sides. "You wanted to attract his attention, didn't you?"

"Yes." Charli pushed away Audrey's hands. "But not everyone else's attention in the joint."

"Well, you gotta let him know what he's missing." Audrey smiled. "The more men who sit up and take notice, the more Connor will notice. You might even kick in a twinge of jealousy."

Jackson studied Charli. "You're right, Charli. It's not quite right." He reached out and grabbed the sides of Charli's jeans and tugged them downward.

"What the hell!" Charli smacked his hands, but before she could pull her jeans back up, Audrey brushed Charli's fingers aside.

"That's it." Audrey nodded. "How about one better?" She slipped her fingers between Charli's belly and the waistband of her low-slung jeans and flipped open the top rivet. "Maybe tease him with a little pubic hair?" Charli's boss laughed, delightedly.

"You'll have me stripping before I walk out of this store-room." Charli held up her finger. "I'm not doing a striptease out there. I told you when I hired on, I can't dance, nor do I want to in front of that bunch of rednecks."

"What about in front of Connor?" Audrey drew a line down the center of Charli's cleavage while her hand dipped into the opening of Charli's jeans. "Bet you'd dance for him. Naked."

Tingles ran across her abdomen. Charli couldn't breathe, her pussy tightening to a point she almost came. "Don't do that, unless you want to share your man," she warned Audrey. "I'm in no mood to be teased and left dry."

"I could be convinced." Audrey's brows rose and she tipped her head to the side. "What about you, Jackson?"

"Ready." He reached for the buttons on his jeans. "Just say the word."

Charli's heart stuttered at the thought of a threesome with Audrey and Jackson, but what would they say to each other afterward? It would all be too weird. She planted her hands on her hips. "Before you get too hot and bothered, what are the other four steps in the hunt?"

"Step two. You have to dangle the bait where the poor slob...er...prey will practically stumble across it." Jackson nuzzled Audrey's neck, moving his mouth up and down her skin. "Um, you smell good."

Still naked from the waist up, Audrey leaned back against Jackson. "Go on."

"And you have beautiful tits," Jackson continued.

Audrey's elbow in his gut set him straight, and he gave Charli a sheepish grin. "Three, Set the Trap." Jackson nipped Audrey's earlobe.

"What do you mean, set the trap?" For a second, she watched her friend's eyelids drift closed then she snapped her fingers in Jackson's face to make him focus.

"Make it your place." Jackson grinned. "Be naked."

"Really?" Audrey frowned. "I'd think a candlelit dinner and a bottle of wine, maybe a sexy negligee that gives a little glimpse of what's beneath without being too revealing."

Jackson chuckled, plumping Audrey's naked breasts. "Simple, honey. Men are simple."

"Four?" Charli's patience had long since thinned. "What about four?"

"Stalk your prey carefully." Jackson's fingers walked up Audrey's arm. "Don't attack right away. Make him sweat."

Be naked when he arrives but don't attack right away? Charli shook her head. "I don't get it."

"Show him a little leg." Audrey's breath caught as Jackson's hand slipped under her waistband. Eyes wide, she hurried to finish with, "Stand in the light so that your outfit becomes see-through, giving him a peek of the treasures beneath."

Jackson glanced up. "Keep it simple."

The tangy scent of aroused female reached Charli's nose and her pussy clenched. "Five?" Charli prompted, her breathing ragged, her body on fire, ready for sex and not sure when she'd be getting any.

"Five is when you've got him where you want him and you go in for the kill. In this case, for the big O. Just remember...naked."

Audrey's back arched and she moaned.

Jackson's finger must have hit the right spot. "Oh, for Pete's sake, get a room." Charli marched for the door, every sexual fantasy she'd lived over the past weeks following her into the saloon, laughing at her, while Jackson's and Audrey's advice swirled in her head.

One thing was certain, if she couldn't get Connor interested while wearing nothing but a pushup bra and a vest, then she'd give up and go back to her vibrator.

Before Charli had gone five feet, Audrey hurried around

her, tugging her t-shirt in place. She grabbed Libby, the bartender, and whispered into her ear. Then a grinning Audrey disappeared back into the store room.

As she stepped out onto the saloon floor, Charli's gaze panned the room, lighting on Connor Mason. He sat at a table near the dance floor, talking to Mark, Luke Gray Wolf and his high school buddy, Ed Judson.

Crap. Why couldn't he be alone? Vamping in front of a table full of his friends wouldn't be easy. But damn it, her pussy ached for some action and she needed to know where she stood with the man.

Squaring her shoulders and sparing a last glance at her plumped cleavage, Charli grabbed a tray and started for the table.

The music on the juke box ended and a new song started, the tune Charli knew all too well. The song that gave every woman hope and filled her with the promise of finding that someone who touched her heart.

Charli groaned and turned back to the bar, biting down on her bottom lip. Should she ignore the music or go for it?

Libby held out a microphone in her direction.

"Really? This song?" Charli set the tray on the wooden bar and snatched the mic from Libby, her heartbeat kicking up a notch, knowing the words as if they had been etched in her brain for all of eternity. The song sung by one of country music's most talented artists. How could Charli, a nobody from Temptation, Texas, begin to measure up? And if she fell short? What if Connor was a big fan of the real artist? What if he didn't like Charli's version?

Self-doubt reared its nasty head, and Charli almost ran from the bar. But the music played on and her need to sing the lyrics made her mouth open. The dance floor cleared and a path opened, allowing her through to the center, directly in front of the table where Connor and his friends sat.

The man next to Connor's whistled at Charli and patted his lap.

Connor glared at him and scooted his chair closer to where Charli stood, giving her his complete attention.

Heat spread through Charli's body. Her voice started out soft, the words filling her, so tender, so gentle, swelling to the refrain. In just a few moments, she stood in the middle of the dance floor, her gaze on Connor, music swirling all around her. She sang the song to him, about him, for him. Her gaze captured his and her chest tightened, the words flowing as if from her heart to his.

When the music ended, another song followed on the juke box and couples moved out onto the dance floor.

Charli stood in a trance, her gaze locked on Connor, unable to form a coherent thought except how much she wanted him to take her in his arms and love her like the lyrics in the song. But Jackson said men were simple. Would Connor get that she'd just poured out her feelings for him, and everyone else, to see? Suddenly, she felt exposed, more so than the stupid vest and bra could begin to reveal. She'd laid open her heart and soul. As fear, embarrassment and emotion welled up inside, Charli's muscles bunched to run.

Then Connor stood, his smoky gaze unfathomable, and he stalked toward her like a panther claiming his territory, joining her on the wooden floor. "Can I have this dance?"

Heart racing, she nodded, all words now locked below the lump in her throat. As she moved into his arms, the need to run transformed into a need to get closer to this special man.

"I knew you could sing...but not like that." His arms tightened around her back. "You have a gift."

In a rush of relief, she laid her face against his chest,

wanting to tell him that she'd sung the song just for him. But she couldn't, the emotion was too new, too raw.

All too soon, the music of the song faded and their feet came to a standstill.

Audrey waved from across the floor, mouthing the words, *Ask him.*

Charli's pulse leaped and she remembered why she'd come onto the main room in the ridiculous outfit in the first place. She leaned back so that she could stare up into Connor's face, into his blue eyes. Blood pounded in her ears as she tried to assemble all that Jackson had taught her into coherent thoughts. Step two, or was it three? Her mouth opened and she blurted, "Will you have sex with me?"

CHAPTER TWELVE

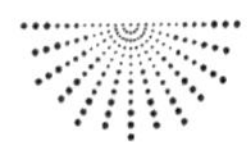

$\mathcal{C}$harli flitted from her bathroom mirror to the front window at least a hundred times as she waited for Connor to arrive. So far, everything was going according to plan. Well, other than asking him outright if he wanted to have sex with her.

Her cheeks burned at the remembered embarrassment and clumsy backpedaling she'd done before she could solicit his commitment for dinner tonight, no pressure to have sex. Though her pussy felt the pressure like nobody's business.

Ever since Charli had danced with Connor on the dance floor, feeling his arms around her as if she was someone precious, she'd been scared.

Scared he'd come, they'd have dinner, and she'd forget how to talk.

Scared he'd find her boring, unattractive and too needy.

Scared the plan would fail, and he'd walk away convinced for the second time that she wasn't worth asking out on another date.

By now, she hadn't gotten a call from her mystery cowboy and she'd gotten to the point she didn't care. Knowing who she was with seemed much more important than living every crazy sexual fantasy she'd ever imagined. Not that the escapades hadn't been hot while they lasted, but, well, the midnight romps weren't something she could build a relationship on. And Charli realized not only did she want sex, she wanted a real, grown-up relationship, with a man who wasn't afraid to show his face.

Still wrapped in a towel, she strode into the bedroom where the pretty figure-hugging deep teal mini-dress lay across her bed. Audrey had loaned it to her for the occasion. Since Charli had blurted out she'd wanted sex, Audrey made the command decision to send a message to Connor that sex wasn't the only thing Charli wanted.

Charli reached for the dress, wondering if the negligee might be the better idea. Jackson had said, keep it simple. No, the dress was gorgeous, she looked gorgeous wearing it and the garment gave her something to strip when the time came. As consolation, she would forgo panties. Knowing how deliciously decadent that would feel as she sat across the table from Connor, eating their intimate dinner. Her body flushed with heat, her pussy dampening.

Maybe he'd run his fingers along her thigh and beneath the dress and discover her secret...

The doorbell rang.

Charli squealed and ran to answer it, realizing as she pulled the door halfway open that she still wore only the towel. A secret smile spread across her face. That was how she'd greeted Connor on their first date.

The sexy Mr. Mason stood there with a broad grin. "Nice."

Her heart pounded. Charli hoped he'd wrap his arms around her like he had the first time, but he didn't.

He winced, his lips twisting. "A buddy of mine from the

military was passing through. I hope you don't mind that I brought him along." With a shuffle, he pulled a man with a short haircut into view.

Charli squealed for the second time, slammed the door shut in their faces and leaned against the wooden panel, a wave of disappointment and panic washing over her. Damn. This wasn't going according to plan at all. "I'll be right back," she called through the door. In less than a minute, she was back, with the dress pulled over her hips. She hadn't had time to find a pair of sexy underwear and barely had time to slip her feet into the high-heeled sandals she'd laid out by her bed.

Yanking open the door, she forced a smile to her face and waved the two men inside her little cottage. "I'm sorry. I wasn't quite ready."

"No apologies necessary. You're beautiful no matter what you wear." Connor lifted her hand to his lips and kissed her fingertips.

Tingles of awareness rippled across Charli's senses and she almost forgot the other man standing by.

His friend chuckled. "Or don't wear."

Connor jabbed him in the ribs. "Forgive my friend. He's been too long in all-male company. He's forgotten his manners."

The tall, broad-shouldered man stuck out a hand. "Grant Bradley. If this is inconvenient, I can leave Connor here and find my own dinner."

"No, no. I made plenty of food. Come in." Charli could have cried. Her plan would have to go on hold while Connor's friend had dinner with them. Maybe having sex with Connor wasn't meant to be. The best she could hope for was getting through the dinner without bursting into tears, or dying of sexual withdrawals.

The men entered the dining room where Charli had the table set for two, with candles, rose petals and her best dishes.

"I'm really sorry. This was obviously a date. I'll just bow out quietly." Grant backed toward the door. "You two have a nice dinner."

"No, really. I'd love for you to stay." Charli reached into her hutch for another plate and laid it on the table.

Dinner passed with laughter and a lot of story swapping, the two men holding up the bulk of the conversation, Charli listening and learning more about Connor than she would, had they been alone. He'd loved the military, had brother-love for the men of his unit and missed it. He came alive when he talked about the missions they'd been on and the danger inherent in a war-torn country. Connor and Grant had shared so much.

Charli couldn't begin to compete with them in a full-blown conversation. She fed them, made sure their glasses were full, and let their voices fill her with a gentle warmth, if not the passionate heat she'd set the "trap" for. Many times she struggled to concentrate when she remembered she wasn't wearing panties beneath the dress, a garment whose skirt was so short it rode up to where a panty-line should have been revealed.

Her heart fluttered as she sat between the two men, her desire growing, despite the conversation all about war.

When she rose to clear the last dish, Connor joined her, carrying his plate into the kitchen. "The chicken cordon bleu was great."

"Yes, it was. Thanks for the home-cooked meal." Grant called out. "Beats the chow hall any day."

As the kitchen door closed between them and Grant, Charli's pulse pounded against the base of her throat. She'd done everything right according to Jackson and Audrey—establishing a pretty trap with the right setting, the right clothing, or lack thereof. With Grant in the other room, Charli could move on to Step Three and stalk her prey. Maybe give him a hint of what he just might be missing.

"Do you think Grant would like coffee?" Charli asked.

"Probably."

When Connor reached around her to rinse his plate in the sink, Charli made her first move. She turned so fast, they stood almost nose-to-nose, her breasts pressing against his chest, her mouth so close to his lips, she could almost taste them. Her heart hammering, she gave a little giggle. "Oops, sorry." Then she ducked under his arm. She'd given him a taste, just a little taste, of what it felt like to get close.

After stowing the dirty dishes in the dishwasher, she busied herself pulling clean spoons from the drawer. When she thought he might be looking her way, Charli leaned up on her toes, stretching an arm high over her head and reaching up into the cabinet where she kept her coffee. She banked on the dress rising up enough to display a healthy portion of her naked ass.

"Look, I appreciate your being so—" Connor's words choked off mid-sentence.

Bingo. Charli cast a glance over her shoulder as she lowered her arm and her dress hem. "I'm sorry, you were saying?"

Connor cleared his throat and continued, his eyes wide and still resting on her hem, now clearly covering her bottom. "—accommodating. Thank you for being so accommodating. Grant would have had to eat by himself."

She turned back to the cabinet for a second time, reaching for the sugar. "He seems nice. Good-looking too."

Rising slowly on her toes, she lifted an arm again, her dress inching upward with the movement...

Connor was behind her in an instant, plucking the sugar from the top shelf. "On second thought, I think Grant isn't into coffee. It's probably time we left."

Charli spun, knocking a coffee mug to the floor where it crashed along with all her hopes of seducing Connor Mason. Ducking her head to hide her shock, she bent to pick up the broken pieces. "Are you sure?"

"What's all the noise in here? Everyone all right?" Grant pushed through the swinging door into the kitchen, his gaze going to where Charli squatted, gathering ceramic shards.

Charli forced a smile. "I was just being clumsy."

Grant grinned. "Are you making coffee?"

"No, she's not." Connor pulled Charli to her feet, brushing at her dress until it covered her thighs. "It's time for us to go. Come on, Grant."

Charli almost laughed at how Connor hurried his buddy out of the kitchen, but the fact they were leaving made her want to shake a fist at her timing and break down and cry. "Are you sure you won't stay?"

Herding his friend toward the front door, Connor grabbed his cowboy hat and plunked it on his head. "Grant needs to get back to my place, he has to leave at the butt-crack of dawn."

Grant nodded. "I have to report in to Ft. Hood in the morning, it's quite a hoof from here."

Charli sighed. "Then I guess you need to get back."

"You know, I'm the only one who has to be somewhere tomorrow." Grant dug in his pocket and pulled out his keys. "If you could give Connor a ride home, he can stay longer."

Charli's chest filled with hope. A perfect solution.

But Connor shook his head, frowning at his friend. "I can't ditch you on your only night in town."

"Who's ditching? I'm not ready to hit the rack, anyway. I thought I'd stop by the Ugly Stick Saloon to catch a dance with that pretty little waitress. What was her name?"

"Which one? They're all pretty." Connor smiled at Charli.

"The brunette with the big brown eyes." Grant tapped his key to his chin. "Bella, I think was her name."

"That's right. The brunette waitress is Bella." Charli's fingers twisted the hem of her skirt, refusing to let her hopes rise yet again only to be crushed so easily.

Connor grabbed her hand, smoothing the skirt down over her thigh, before facing his friend. "If you're sure? I think Mark and Luke will be there. You know them."

"I know how to get around in a bar by myself. Don't you worry, man. Enjoy." Grant winked at Charli and left, pulling the door closed behind him with a snap.

For a long moment, she and Connor stared at the door, unmoving.

He was first to break the silence. "Are you wearing any underwear?"

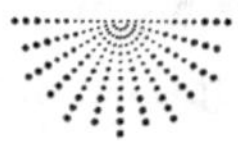

harli's fingers tightened in his, heat flowing through her body like molten lava, spreading low to that suddenly drenched place between her thighs. "No."

Connor spun her into his arms, lifted up her legs, wrapping them around his waist and pressed her up against the wall. "All through dinner, were you wearing any underwear?" he asked, his blue-eyed gaze boring into hers.

She shook her head, her glance dropping to his lips only inches from hers. Her tongue darted out dampening suddenly dry lips, her pussy resting on the ridge pressing against his denim fly, the coarse fabric setting off electrical shocks that couldn't be ignored. "Does that bother you?"

He groaned, his mouth crushing hers in a soul-stealing kiss, his fingers digging into her naked ass. "It bothers me a lot," he said, into her mouth as his tongue lashed out, twisting around hers.

When Connor came up for air, Charli rested her arms on his shoulders, ready to launch the final step in Jackson's hunting scenario—the kill. "So what are you doing about the situation?"

"This." He lifted her, carried her into her bedroom and laid her out on her bed, spreading her legs wide. "We'll start here." Dropping to his knees, he draped her knees over his shoulders and pulled her bottom to the edge, his tongue diving into her pussy, swirling around and around in her juices. His fingers parted her folds, laying open the little nubbin of swollen nerve-endings, pulsing with every heart-beat. Licking his way up to her clit, he sucked it into his mouth, tugging at the skin, nipping gently before flicking it again and again.

Charli's fingers dug into the comforter, her back arching off the mattress, as the tingling sensations spread from the tips of her fingers and toes, working their way inward to implode in a cataclysmic burst of sensations. Within seconds, she rocketed to the moon in the most earth-shattering orgasm she'd ever experienced."Oh, dear God, I'm dying," she cried as her body stiffened and she rode the intense wave, cresting and sliding into shore on a sigh. After what felt like hours, but had only been moments, she sank back to earth, her body quivering, her insides a mass of fractured nerves.

A chuckle warmed her skin. Connor slid her up on the bed and lay down between her legs, still fully clothed.

Stretching, she reached for the buttons on his jeans, flipping open the top one with a desperation she'd only begun to realize. "I want you inside me."

He smoothed a hand across her cheek, tucking a strand of hair behind her ears. "Soon."

"Now." The tigress in her refused to be put off another moment. Too much time had been wasted waiting. She pushed him to his back and tore through the buttons on his shirt, none too gently, popping one free of the thread. The round disk pinged against the headboard and bounced off the nightstand.

Charli didn't care. She could sew it back on later. Once she had his shirt open, she laid her cheek against his chest, his warmth stirring her desire back to life, keeping it from fading into delicious afterglow. She grabbed the waistband of his jeans and tugged the remaining buttons free, wanting to see what he had to offer, knowing she wouldn't be disappointed, based on the size of the ridge.

His dick sprang free, popping to attention, hard, thick and long.

Charli's pussy pulsed, aching for him to fill her, to thrust deep inside.

But first, she wanted to give him what he'd given her.

She tugged the jeans down his legs, admiring trim hips and well-muscled thighs, covered in curly, manly hairs. Her hands skimmed across him, reveling in the hard planes and defined ridges of muscles and sinew.

Leaning up on his elbows, he shrugged the shirt down his arms, tossed it to the corner and reached for his jeans before she could throw them to the floor. "Wait." He pulled his wallet from his back pocket and slipped a foil packet from inside.

Charli laughed. "I'd completely forgotten." She plucked the packet from his fingers and laid it on the pillow beside his head. "Later." She gave him what she hoped was a sexy smile and went down on him, sliding her pussy over one of his thighs, leaving a slippery trail of come. Then she wrapped her hands around his length, enjoying the steely velvet of warm skin and desire. With a sigh, she dragged her cheek across his head, touching her tongue to his tip, tapping into the hole, already primed with lust.

Her mouth closed around the bulbous head, sliding down over him, taking his length as far as she could, until he bumped against the back of her throat. As she slid back to the top, she glanced up at his face, gauging his reaction.

A self-satisfied warmth spread through Charli's chest as Connor's fingers clutched at the comforter, the tightness of his jaw and the fire gleaming in his eyes, spurred her on. She settled into a rhythm, sinking down over him and back up, slowly at first, teasing, testing his reaction.

He reached for her hips, spinning her around, sliding one of her knees over his head to position her pussy over his mouth.

Then the fun began anew.

As she worked his cock, sucking hard, scraping her teeth softly along his length, she massaged his balls between her fingers.

Connor grabbed her hips and spread her knees wider until his tongue could flick at her clit.

A charged jolt of electricity zipped through her, singing her nerves, sending wave upon wave of sensations skittering through her body, pooling in her molten-hot core.

Her fingers curled around his hips and she shoved him deep into her mouth, taking him all the way in as his tongue thrust into her cunt.

It couldn't get better than when she blitzed to her second orgasm of the night.

Suddenly Connor flung her to the mattress on her back, ripped open the foil and rolled the condom down over his cock. He shoved a knee between hers and dropped down to where his cock nudged her opening. "I can't wait any longer."

His gruff words brought a smile to her lips. "Good." Her legs wrapped around his waist and she dug her heels into his buttocks as he thrust deep inside her, hard and fast, stretching and filling her channel until his balls slammed against her ass.

Charli gasped, her back arching off the bed.

Connor pulled back, his eyes wide. "Did I hurt you?"

"God, no," she whispered, digging her heels into his buttocks once more. "Again!" He rammed into her again, thrusting deep, his thickness almost more than she could bear and yet, richly erotic and completely satisfying.

Over and over he pushed into her, thrusting, retreating and thrusting again until his gorgeous, naked skin gleamed with perspiration and he froze.

Barely able to breathe, Charli stared up at his face.

Connor's jaw tightened to stone and he threw back his head as he thrust once more, then held still, his member pulsing inside Charli.

When at last he looked back down at her, a smile spread across his lips. "You're amazing."

"You're not so bad yourself." As the intensity of her orgasm eased, she reached up to cup his cheek. "Why in hell did we wait to do this?"

He rolled with her to his side, maintaining the intimate connection, pulling her into the curve of his muscled arm. "I'm a one-woman kind of guy. I wanted to be sure you were a one-man kind of girl." Connor kissed her and smoothed his hands through her hair and whispered sweet nothings into her ear. Eventually, the cowboy fell into a deep sleep.

Charli lay for a long time in his arms, knowing this was exactly where she wanted to be, but not knowing if she was what Connor needed. Their dates had occurred at the same time she was seeing her mystery cowboy. A niggle of discomfort, maybe even guilt, nagged at her subconscious. She had to end it once and for all with Original Sin. The sooner the better. But how could she break it off with him when she didn't even have his phone number?

And should she tell Connor about her previous love life?

His statement of "a one-man kinda gal" hinted he'd be shocked as hell at her actions. *Don't spoil this night.*

Warm and satiated from the most mind-blowing sex she'd had in her entire life, Charli stayed awake through most of the night, not knowing what to do next.

LIGHT STREAMED through the gap in the wooden blinds, the beam falling across the rumpled sheets, warming Charli Sutton's skin. She stretched, her eyes blinking open to the brightness of the room. A glance at the clock confirmed the time was near noon. She'd never slept better.

Charli yawned, pushed hair out of her face and ran a hand down her neck to her naked breasts, and froze. Eyes widening, a flood of memories washed over her, heating her body, sending fiery signals of lust straight to her pussy.

"Connor," she whispered, her eyes darting to the pillow beside her. Instead of the studly cowboy, Connor Mason, a crisp white piece of paper lay in the gentle indention where his head had lain. On top of the paper lay a deep red rose from Charli's own garden.

Her insides churning, Charli sat up straight, disappointment her first reaction, knowing the note meant he'd gone. And she'd had such a rush of needs overwhelming her, she'd hoped he'd be there to satisfy them or at least take the edge off before she faced the day.

Had to go to work. I'll see you at the Cowboy Masquerade Ball tonight.

Charli clutched the note to her chest and cupped the rose beneath her nose, the warmth of hope filling her.

He wanted to see her again.

She sank back against the pillow, a smile curling her lips.

Connor had been so gentle and yet forceful making love, not once, but several times throughout the night.

A delicious ache centered at her entrance where the friction of his thrusts had send her reeling over the edge of orgasm more than once. His lips had seared a path from hers all the way down her throat, skimming across the swells of her breasts.

Charli trailed the rose along the side of her neck and downward to the tip of one nipple. The areola drew tight in response, still sensitive from the burn of Connor's beard. She circled the tip with the velvety smooth petals, spurring longing deep inside, tugging at her core, sending waves of cream-filled desire to her pussy.

She moaned and squirmed beneath the rose, sliding it lower still, across her ribs, skimming past her bellybutton to the furry mound at the apex of her thighs.

His lips had been there too, his fingers parting her folds, exposing that little bud of nerves, ripe and pulsing, ready for whatever sweet torture he had in mind.

Charli's heels dug into the mattress, just as they had when Connor spread her knees wide and laid down between her legs, gathering her bottom in his big, calloused hands, lifting her pussy to his lips.

The flower brushed lower, slipping past her dampened pussy, tickling the insides of her thighs. She let her knees fall open, the cool morning air kissing the moisture pooling in her vagina. With one hand, she brushed the rose across her cunt, with the other, she dipped a finger into the heated wetness, sliding it up to her clit bringing a thick coating of come.

Not as powerful as Connor's tongue, but good in a pinch.

She closed her eyes and remembered how it felt to have his mouth on her, licking and teasing, flicking her most receptive erogenous zone, blinding her with such a bright array of sensations she thought she might die from over-exposure.

Her finger tapped her clit then slathered it in moisture.

Connor had licked her, swirling his tongue around and around, shooting spurts of adrenaline and desire through her bloodstream. As it was now, the tingling began in her outer extremities, traveling with lightning speed to her center.

Charli moaned, her back arching off the bed, the speed with which she stroked her clit increasing until the pleasure bordered on pain. Her finger stilled, her hand cupping her pussy pressed down, until the orgasm peaked, the sheer beauty of the sensation bursting through to brighten the midday sun.

As she fell back to earth, Charli sighed, pulling up the sheets over her breasts. She dragged the pillow Connor had used against her body in a poor imitation of the solidly built, muscular cowboy. She'd much rather awaken to the real man, making love to her body.

Maybe next time. She grinned and squealed into the pillow. Connor Mason had finally made love to her, and the experience had been everything she'd hoped and dreamed of.

As the rest of the night came back to her, his final comment before she'd drifted off to sleep came back to haunt her.

I'm a one-woman kind of guy. I wanted to be sure you were a one-man kind of girl.

The beauty of the day faded into a pall of guilt and worry.

Charli had been dating Connor while seeing a mystery cowboy after midnight. Granted, she'd never said she was going to date Connor exclusively when it all started between the two of them. And she still didn't know who her mystery cowboy was. At this point, that fact barely mattered. She hadn't seen the stranger in a week, nor did she care to. Connor was the man for her. He was gentle, kind, a war hero, a sexy cowboy and now...she knew without a shadow of a doubt, he was great in bed.

What more could a woman ask for?

Charli flopped back against her own pillow. What would happen if he found out about the mystery cowboy? Should she tell him and get it over with? Her chest squeezed at the thought. What if he dumped her? What if he said he couldn't be with a woman who kept things from him?

Chewing on her lip, Charli weighed her options and came up short. Her conscience wouldn't let her live a lie. Not when she stood a chance at a real relationship with a great guy. If they couldn't be honest with each other, where did that leave them?

She rolled over and hugged the pillow. Oh, but he'd been so sweet, so kind, so... hunki-licious. How could she live without him, now that she'd tasted what he had to offer? Another groan and Charli sat up, pushing the pillow and sheets aside.

The only way to deal with an impossible situation was to meet it head-on. But she could always face the challenge looking her best. Tonight was the Cowboy Masquerade Ball —a tradition at the Ugly Stick Saloon to sponsor a masquerade ball for the locals and the rodeo cowboys, after the first day of the rodeo events. Her boss, Audrey Andersen, always insisted her girls dress in costumes, usually those of old-time dancehall girls.

A satisfied smile spread across Charli's face. Good. She looked great in a corset bustier and the flouncy skirts only showed off her legs. How could he possibly dump her when she'd be displaying her best assets?

She snatched her phone from the nightstand and started

to dial Audrey's number for someone to talk to about the night past and the night ahead. One glance at the clock on the wall reminded her that Audrey slept in after working until the small hours of the morning. But Charli had to talk to someone. She hit the speed-dial button for her friend, Mona Daley, Temptation's most gifted beautician.

"Shear Safari, this is Mona."

"Mona!" Charli exclaimed. "Please tell me you can fit me in today."

"Charli?" Mona laughed. "Mrs. Smith just cancelled; her slot is yours if you can make it here in ten minutes. What's up?"

"I'll tell you when I get there. Suffice it to say, I need you…desperately."

"I'll polish the shampoo bowl and warm the curling irons. See ya in a few, sweetie."

Charli washed her face, brushed her teeth, threw on jeans and a tank top and crammed a straw cowboy hat on her head to hide her tousled hair. Just in case she ran into anyone important on her way to the salon. As she backed out of her driveway and shifted into drive, her body tingled all over at the thought of running into Connor in Temptation. Not that she would. He'd be working out at the O'Brien ranch today or helping out with the rodeo. Still, the mere thought of seeing him again after the night they'd shared had her hot and bothered by the time she arrived on Main Street at the Shear Safari Hair Salon.

She glanced in her rearview mirror, a movement catching her attention. A tall, broad-shouldered man in a black Stetson was entering the hardware store behind her.

A gasp escaped her throat. The sight of the black cowboy hat set Charli's heart thumping and she flung open her door, dropping down out of her pickup onto the pavement, ready to chase after the man. She would have, if Mona hadn't chosen that exact moment to poke her head out the salon door.

"Hurry, Charli, I only have an hour for you and I want to hear everything." Mona held open the door.

Torn between chasing after a man in a black Stetson who could possibly be her mystery lover, Original Sin, and Mona, standing there, expecting her to rush in and make her day with a full recounting of her sensuous escapades with Connor, Charli turned toward the salon.

Then man in the black Stetson couldn't be her Original Sin. Since she hadn't heard from him in almost a week, she figured he had to have left town. Besides, what would she do if she went up to the man in the cowboy hat? She couldn't ask him if he was the man who'd fucked her in the Judge's pool or the one who staged a roadblock to entertain her with a ménage à trois on the side of the highway. How could she confront him about the formal dinner in the furniture store with dessert being three men making love to her? And don't forget the BDSM with four guys in the county jail museum.

"Wow, Charli, are you feeling okay? Your face is flushed." Mona pressed a hand to Charli's forehead.

"I'm fine." Charli brushed Mona's hand to the side and walked straight for the shampoo bowl, tossing her cowboy hat in a vacant chair. "I have no idea where to begin."

Mona motioned toward the bowl. "We can begin by washing your hair. You know how the shampooing relaxes you."

Charli plunked in the chair and leaned back.

Mona turned on the water and adjusted the temperature. "I was feeling very neglected. It's been more than two weeks since we last talked, what's been going on?"

"Besides dirty tricks with a complete stranger and a love

affair with Connor Mason? Not much." Charli's pulse raced as she divulged the happenings of the past ten days. "I can't believe only ten days have passed since I first complained about being bored in Temptation."

Mona whistled. "Dang, girl, are you still bored?"

"No!" Charli squeezed shut her eyes and pinched the bridge of her nose, feeling a headache coming on. "My head's been spinning and I don't know what to do. That's why I'm here. I need advice."

"Okay, shoot."

"What should I do?"

"About mystery man or Connor?"

"Both."

"Which one do you love?"

Charli recalled the tender yet aggressive lover she'd had in Original Sin and his willingness to sweeten the pot with additional lovers thrown in the mix. They'd shared a mad and crazy adventure for four nights straight.

But then Connor had taken his time, wooing her, talking to her as if she meant more to him than a piece of ass. He'd shown her respect and courtesy, holding off on making love until she'd pushed past his defenses and taunted him into crossing the line. Now that she'd made love to Connor…

Mona's hands stopped scrubbing Charli's scalp and she tsked. "Oh, baby doll, that was supposed to be an easy answer."

"I love what Original Sin did with me. He got my blood flowing again, awakening desires and showing me the possibilities and opportunities for adventure available even in such a small town as Temptation." Charli sighed. "On the other hand…Connor…" She signed again.

"He's hot." Mona's fingers dug in, scrubbing again. Then

she rinsed. "If you decide not to commit to Connor, can I have him?"

Heat shot through her chest, and Charli's fingernails dug into the chair's arms. "Hands off. Connor's mine."

Mona stepped back, holding up her dripping hands. "Okay, no need to bite off my head." She grinned and winked. "I guess that answers it."

"Answers what?"

"You're in love with Connor."

"I just wish I could have both. The surprise and spontaneity of my mystery lover was off-the-charts hot. Then again, Connor knows just the right spots to hit to launch me over the edge."

"You can stop this minute. I'm creaming and horny now, and I have a busy day of appointments to get through before I can do anything about it."

Charli grabbed Mona's wrist. "You have to be there at the Ugly Stick tonight. I don't know if I can manage on my own."

"Don't worry, honey. I have my costume all ready. I wouldn't miss the Cowboy Masquerade Ball for anything." Mona wrapped Charli's hair in a towel and leaned her forward in the chair.

Charli moved to Mona's station and sat in the swivel chair. "Now, make me so beautiful, Connor can't help but fall in love with me."

"Speaking of Connor…" Mona nodded toward the large picture window looking out over Main Street. "Isn't that him coming out of Lisenby's Jewelry Store?" Her hands resting on Charli's shoulders squeezed hard. "Oh my gosh. He's carrying a bag."

Charli spun in her chair. Just as Mona had said, Connor was walking away from the jewelry store with a small bag. Her heart skipped several beats then raced ahead. "Oh, my."

She grabbed Mona's hands, her own shaking. "Do something!"

Mona laughed. "Do what?"

"Make me gorgeous." Charli braced herself as if preparing for major surgery.

Starting with a brush, Mona stroked through the damp hair, smoothing it straight, the ends curling naturally. "Is Audrey using the saloon girl costumes again?"

"I suppose." Dear Lord, what was she going to do...what was she going to say? And what in heaven had Connor bought at the jewelry store? A ring, maybe?

Charli's stomach flipped and landed with a thump.

Mona's hands settled on her shoulders. "It's going to be okay. But just to give you confidence to face the night, let's give you a go-to-hell hairstyle that will have all the men drooling over you...one in particular."

Charli forced herself to relax back in the seat as Mona did her magic. All the while the beautician worked, Charli alternated between breathing normally and a full-on panic attack. What if Connor Mason had purchased an engagement ring? Holy crap. She could be getting engaged that very night.

Mona hugged her and whispered in her ear, "Breathe, Charli. Breathe."

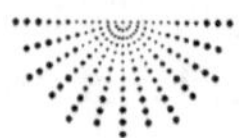

Charli stepped out of the Shear Safari feeling like a million dollars. Her talk with Mona had helped calm her, and the hairstyle creation Mona dreamed up looked fabulous. Sexy, sassy and perfect for the Cowboy Masquerade Ball. Charli couldn't wait to see Connor's reaction when she was in costume tonight. He had to fall madly in love with her, if he wasn't already.

She stopped on the sidewalk, her hand pressing against her left breast where her heart squeezed hard. Was she in love with Connor? Could she be ready to take the next step after only two dates with the man? The thought of him proposing sent tingles down her spine at the same time as her breath caught in her throat. She wanted him. Oh, man, she wanted him. But did she want him forever?

As she stared off into the distance, another tall, broad-shouldered man in a black Stetson passed by in her peripheral vision.

By the time Charli turned her head, he'd disappeared, leaving her to wonder whether or not he'd been a figment of her imagination. She shook her head, pasted a smile on her face and strutted down the street, swinging her cowboy hat in her hand, afraid wearing it would mess up her new 'do. She had a stop to make at the drug store for condoms and lubricant. If tonight went as planned, she'd be using the whole box and tube.

Temptation was teaming with cowboys and their support crews for the annual Tri-County Rodeo. Trucks towing fancy horse trailers rumbled along Main Street, loaded to the gills with hay, tack, feed sacks and their most precious cargo —horses.

Cowboys waved and called out to each other, having ridden the circuit and studied up on their competition. They strutted by in their blue jeans and snap shirts, displaying their biggest, shiniest belt buckles won at the various rodeos across the country and into Canada.

Charli hadn't gone ten steps without passing five good-looking men, each tipping their cowboy hats in her direction. She smiled and said hello, friendly, but not too friendly. Then a cowboy with sky blue eyes, medium brown hair and a black Stetson strode by, tipped his hat and winked.

Her heart leaping to her throat, Charli tripped over her own cowboy boots and almost plowed face-first into a streetlight pole.

The cowboy reached out and steadied her, his hand going around her waist, warm and rough.

With her mouth open to ask him if he was her lover, Charli didn't get out the words before Sadie Watkins burst from the drugstore, waving a bag. "Mr. Sanders, you forgot your wife's medication!"

"Are you all right?" The tall, dark and married cowboy still held her elbow.

Heat rose up Charli's neck and into her cheeks as she thanked the heavens she hadn't blurted out what had been poised on her lips. "I'm fine, just clumsy." She stepped away, until his hand fell to his side. "Thanks."

The man tipped his hat and smiled at Sadie. "Thanks, miss. Julia would skin me alive if I came back empty handed." He tipped his hat at Sadie, smiled at Charli and strode toward a very large pickup truck.

Not until he got in and backed away from the curb did Charli gather her senses and dive into the drugstore. Sadie waved, a grin spreading across her face. "Mister Sanders has a way of making a girl's knees weak, doesn't he?" She sighed. "Why are all the good ones taken?"

"I don't know. But seems there are a bunch of them out on the streets today."

Sadie rolled her eyes. "Rodeo clowns all of them. A girl in every town, and probably the STD's to go with them. What can I do for you? Your hair looks fabulous, by the way."

For the second time in as many minutes, Charli's face flushed with heat. "Thanks, Sadie. I had a few things I needed to get." She hurried toward the shelf full of condoms and tubes of lubricating jellies and stood for a long time, searching for those "things". She wondered if her mystery cowboy had arrived early in Temptation to prepare for the rodeo. And why were there so many kinds of condoms, and which ones should she choose? The selection seemed endless.

Sadie appeared at her side. "Crazy choices, aren't there? I have troubles deciding as well. It really depends on what your man likes. Does he have a preference?"

Having already spilled her guts to two of her friends about her sexual exploits, Charli couldn't tell another soul. Sadie was nice enough, but if word got out to the town gossips, the news would be all over Temptation that Charli Sutton was a slut, sleeping with multiple partners. If that got to Connor before she had a chance to explain…Holy crap.

"I'm getting these for a friend," Charli lied.

Sadie smiled, nodding, as if to say yeah, sure, that's what they all say. "If you're not certain, try these." She plucked a box off the shelf. "They're ribbed to give the woman a little more thrill, and they fit comfortably for the man of a larger size, if you know what I mean." Sadie winked.

"Thanks." Charli snatched the box from Sadie's hands. "I'm sure she'll like it."

"Like them or not, at least you'll be protected."

Charli started to reiterate that the condoms weren't for her, but decided against it, figuring Sadie got that response a lot, and who cared? Charli was getting some after a long dry spell. She should consider that fact cause to celebrate.

Sadie turned toward the checkout stand. "I can take you at register one whenever you're ready. Take your time."

Charli selected a lubricating jelly and wandered into the makeup department for new eyeliner and eye shadow to go with her costume and mask for the Cowboy Masquerade Ball. At the counter, she laid out her selections.

Sadie scanned the items without commenting on any of them.

With a sigh, Charli relaxed. Everything would work out all right. As soon as she saw Connor tonight, she'd tell him about her sexual exploits and assure him that they were over. Not having heard from Original Sin in what was going on six days now, what were the chances he'd show up in her life tonight of all nights?

Sadie slid her purchases into a plastic bag and handed back her credit card . "I'll see you at the ball, tonight?"

With a smile, Charli nodded. "I'm working it. Look for the harried saloon girl slinging drinks."

"Watch for me, I'm coming as Belle Starr. Even found a plastic Colt revolver and holster to wear with my dress."

"You'll be beautiful, but you might get frisked at the door, especially if you're packing."

Sadie grinned. "Oooh, you really think so? That would be fine with me as long as it's not Greta Sue. Give me one of the hunks and I'm all for a little foreplay." The clerk's laughter followed Charli out the door.

Her steps lighter, Charli hurried toward her car, ready to get home, take a nap and rinse off before she reported for bartending duty at the Ugly Stick this evening. They'd be open extra late with the festivities of the ball, so a little rest wouldn't hurt. And if Connor stayed late as well…She hugged the bag of condoms and lubricant close.

A brightly painted SUV stood in front of her little cottage with the words Sweet Temptation's Florist painted in hot-pink scrolling letters.

Charli pulled into her driveway and got out, tucking her bag of purchases close to her side.

"Hey, Charli." Bunny Leigh bounced out of the driver's seat and waved. Then she rounded to the rear hatch, opened it and retrieved a large bouquet of yellow roses mixed with happy white daisies. "These are for you."

Charli stopped, her empty hand going to her chest. "For me? Who sent them?"

"Don't know. Whoever purchased them called in the order while I was in the back. The name might be on the card." Bunny extended the bouquet. "Careful, they're heavy. It's one of my favorite bouquets, yet."

"It's lovely." Charli's eyes filled with tears. She'd never received such a beautiful array of posies. "You're really good, Bunny. Thanks." Anxious to get inside and tear into the little yellow envelope sticking out of the middle of the arrangement, Charli hurried up the steps. She set the flowers on the porch and unlocked the door, scooping the flowers up into her arm and rushing inside.

Once in the kitchen, she dropped the bag and the vase on the counter and ripped the envelope from the plastic holder. Inside was a single flat card with words written in bold print.

Love you naked.

Charli flipped over the card, searching for a signature, initials, anything that would indicate who had sent them. Panic made her turn over the card several more times until she gave up and told herself the sender had to be Connor. He was the last man to see her naked.

"Hey, beautiful." A deep rumbling voice sounded behind Charli.

She spun, the hand clutching the card pressed against her chest. "Oh, Connor! You scared the crap out of me."

He smiled.

His blue eyes melted Charli's knees.

"The front door was open, and when I knocked on the frame, no answer, so here I am." He held out a bunch of pretty red roses. "These are for you."

Charli reached for them, the card still in her clenched fist, too many thoughts winging through her head to make sense. "Th-thank you."

Connor's gaze moved past her to the flowers on the counter, a frown pulling his brows together. "Nice." He glanced her way. "Should I be jealous?"

Charli swallowed hard, the lump in her throat settling into her belly. "Uh, no. No, not at all." She thought quickly. "I have a friend at the florist." True, but not the whole truth, unless Bunny had swung the other way and loved her naked.

"Oh, well. In that case…" Connor hooked her elbow and dragged her into his arms, crushing the flowers and the note card between them. "I'm on an errand in town and, since I didn't get to give you a proper good morning kiss, I thought I'd stop by."

His lips descended over Charli's, warm, sensuous and oh, so wonderful. She melted into his arms, losing herself in his embrace, heat building low in her belly, her pussy dampening as his tongue slid between her teeth and claimed hers.

When he lifted his head, Connor gave a husky laugh. "I should have known a kiss wouldn't be enough." He set her away from his body and stared down at the bulge in his jeans. "You make me crazy."

Still clutching the flowers, Charli forced a laugh past her kiss-swollen lips. "Not nearly as much as you make me."

"I should go." He held out his hand for hers.

Charli reached for him with the hand still holding the card.

"What's this?" Connor touched the paper lodged between her fingers.

Charli's heartbeat fluttered against her ribs, and she jerked her hand behind her back. "Just a note to myself." She fought to keep from freaking out. What if he demanded to see the note? Obviously, he hadn't sent the flowers, leaving Original Sin as the mystery sender and penman of the Love you naked note.

"Let me see." Connor held out his hand.

Her first instinct was to shove the note into her mouth and swallow it to keep Connor from discovering her secret. But sure as she tried, she'd choke on it, he'd have to save her, she'd be embarrassed and he'd see the note all nasty and damp anyway.

Charli reached out with her empty hand and pulled Connor close. "I missed you, too." She slipped her hand behind him, sliding it into his back jeans pocket, tugging him closer until the ridge of his fly dug into her belly. "Any chance your lunch break is long enough to take up where we left off?" She wiggled her hips, rubbing him suggestively.

His fingers curled around her waist and he held her still. "Don't, unless you mean it."

What had started as a ploy to distract his attention from the note had blown into full-fledged lust. Charli's body burned so hot she feared her clothes would catch fire. Suddenly she couldn't wait to get out of them and strip Connor naked. "I mean it. Can you tell me that you can wait until three or four o'clock in the morning to do this?" Charli stepped back, her fingers going to the buttons on her shirt, flicking them open one at a time. She led him toward her bedroom, her shirt falling to the floor.

"I really should get back to work. I have a lot to do…" Connor's voice faced off as Charli's fingers closed around the rivet at the waistband of her jeans. "Then again…" He took one step forward.

Charli's smile broadened and she flipped free the rivet. "Fifteen minutes, that's all I'm asking. Otherwise it'll be the tiny hours of tomorrow morning before you see me like this again."

Connor's gaze rested on Charli's fingers as she slid down the zipper, exposing the black lace thong beneath. His Adam's apple rose and fell as he swallowed hard. "I guess I could spare fifteen minutes." He took another step, then another.

"You have to catch me first." Charli shimmied out of her jeans, turned and ran for the bedroom, excitement bubbling up in her veins, a giggle rising from her throat.

"Game on," Connor said behind her, a thud of a boot hitting the floor followed by another before socked feet pounded down the hallway after her.

He caught her at the foot of her bed, lifted her in the air, kissed her soundly, and then tossed her on the mattress.

Charli squealed as she landed then assumed what she hoped was a sexy pose, wearing nothing but the black thong and her best black lace bra. "Is that all you have, cowboy?"

Fingers slipping the buttons free on his shirt, Connor stalked around the side of the bed. "There's more...so much more." He shed his shirt, letting it fall to the floor. In the next second, he was on the bed, lying beside her, kissing her, his tongue thrusting between her teeth, teasing hers, sliding along its length.

It wasn't enough. She wanted him inside her, thrusting his cock in the same motion as his tongue. Her blood pounded through her veins, her breath catching in her throat.

His mouth left hers, traveling down the edge of her jaw, following the line of her throat, kissing and nipping at the sensitized skin until he found the puckered nipples pressing against the silken, lacey fabric of her bra. He bit through the lace, capturing a nipple below, rolling it between his teeth.

Charli's back arched off the mattress, a moan escaping past her vocal cords. "More. Please, more."

"For you...anything." He pushed her bra over her breasts, then sucked a nipple deep into his mouth, pulling hard.

Her feet digging into the mattress, Charli pressed upward, her hands capturing his head, holding him close as wave after wave of sensation washed over her.

Connor's other hand tweaked the tip of her other nipple, then slid across her ribs and downward.

"Oh, Connor, hurry, before I come apart." Charli's fingers gripped his hair, urging him downward.

He complied, leaving a trail of warm, wet kisses across her ribs and down to her panty line. His thumbs hooked the elastic and dragged the black lace over her mound and down her legs to her ankles.

Impatient for more, Charli kicked off the panties, slinging them to a corner.

A grin spread across Connor's face and he crept up the middle of the bed between her legs, his hand sliding along the inside of her thigh to the center of her heat.

Charli lifted her knees then let them fall to the side, exposing her wet core to Connor.

He bent his head, leaving butterfly kisses on the insides of both knees and all the way up to her pussy.

"Please, Connor, please," Charli begged. "You're teasing me."

"I thought you liked foreplay." His tongue flicked out, swirling around her channel, delving in then back out.

Charli gasped. "It's highly overrated," she said, her breath catching as her muscles clenched in response to his next attack on her vagina.

"I think it's well worth the effort." He parted the hairs over her clit, then the folds and breathed out a warm stream of air.

The sparks the air ignited made Charli buck beneath him. "Please, Connor, make me scream."

His chuckle added more warm air to her already heated pussy.

"Nooowwww," she cried out.

"Patience, sweetheart." He tongued her clit, laving her like a tasty morsel, licking and sucking the nubbin into his mouth.

Charli's fingers dug into Connor's hair, her nails scraping against his scalp, the sensations rocketing through her, launching her into orgasm. She threw back her head and screamed, her body pulsing, each spasm racking over her until she fell back against the bed, completely limp.

Chuckling, Connor crawled up her body, his bare chest pressing against her breasts, his jeans scraping against her thighs and hips.

"Aren't you overdressed?" Charli reached between them, her fingers finding the rivet at his waistline.

His hand stopped her and he kissed the tip of her nose. "I can wait." He kissed her lips. "I have to get back to work. I promised the boss I'd help out at the rodeo. Gabe's bronc riding today."

Disappointment welled up. "Really? You're leaving?" She wriggled against him. "Sure you don't want to stay?"

"Oh, I want to stay." He kissed her soundly and rolled off the bed. "But I have to go."

Body still languid with afterglow, Charli slipped her bra in place, sat up and drew her knees up to her chin. "I'll see you tonight?"

He shoved his arms into his shirt, his boots on his feet and crammed his cowboy hat on his head. "Save a dance for me." With a wink, he left.

For a long moment, Charli sat there, her pussy still throbbing, aching for Connor, the aftermath of her orgasm still rippling through her system. Then she flopped back, turned and buried her face in a pillow and screamed her frustration, pounding her fists against the mattress.

After her little burst of frustration, she lay there for a long moment, buried in her pillows, a thousand thoughts roiling around her mind, all coming back to her safe, sensitive cowboy, Connor Mason and the fact that she'd had the opportunity to tell him about her mystery cowboy and hadn't.

Damn.

That night, she'd tell him. She'd pull him to the side and break it to him, first thing.

Her cell phone buzzed on her nightstand several times before she pulled her face out of the pillows and snatched it up, praying the caller was Connor, asking her to let him back in to finish what they'd started. Then maybe she'd tell him what she should have told him already.

The buzzing stopped before she could answer and the caller ID indicated an unknown caller.

Charli's heart skipped several beats then raced ahead as the light blinked on for a voice mail message. She eased her finger onto the play button.

"Hi, beautiful. Ready for our next dirty trick?"

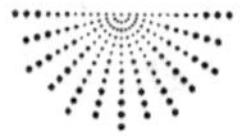

Charli paced in the storeroom, only half-listening while Audrey gave her instructions to the waitresses before the doors opened on the Ugly Stick Saloon, and the annual Cowboy Masquerade Ball commenced. She'd done the best she could to fix her mussed hair, finally piling it up on top of her head in careless curls. The tumble in the bed with Connor had been well worth destroying Mona's handiwork.

Customers lined up out front, waiting to get in, many wearing costumes, others would be given black masks as they entered to allow them to join in the masquerade, should they choose.

Normally excited by the hoopla, Charli was already sweating the hoards of cowboys that would descend on the saloon in moments. Tonight would be a nightmare, an absolute nightmare.

The call she'd received shortly after Connor left her, still horny and a little less than satisfied, had been from her AWOL mystery cowboy, who'd proceeded to drop the bomb. He'd been sorry about being out of touch, but that he planned to make it up to her. That night he'd be wearing a black cowboy hat and wearing a yellow rose at the ball.

The same night Connor would be there, and Charli still hadn't told him the truth.

"Charli, honey, are you all right?" Bella Severs slipped an arm around Charli's waist. "You're as wound up as a blind rattlesnake getting her new button."

"I'm just a little worried." Charli appreciated the hug. She could use a lot of those right now, when her world stood a chance of falling completely apart. But the longer Bella hugged her, the more she felt trapped. She turned her back to the pretty brunette. "Could you pull the strings on this corset just a bit tighter? I'd hate to have it come undone during our number."

"Why worry? The cowboys would love it." Lacey Neil skimmed her finger along the top of Charli's black corset. "I'd love it too. You have lovely breasts."

"Don't listen to her," Kendall Mason called out from the other side of Audrey. "She'll be giving you sex education lessons before you know it, and then all hell will break loose."

Lacey pouted toward her former housemate, Kendall. "You know you loved it. Admit it."

Kendall grinned. "You bet. And the best part is that I got my cowboy."

Bella tugged on the strings at Charli's back. "Just rub it in, why don't you? Ed Judson is quite a catch. I wouldn't mind having him give me a few sex education lessons as well."

"Watch it." Kendall's eyes narrowed. "He's all mine. Plenty of cowboys are out there tonight for you to choose from, so keep your paws off my man." Her words sounded harsher than the smile on her face belied.

"Wouldn't do you any good anyway, Ed's only got eyes for Kendall." Audrey glanced around at the women assembled.

She wore a similar dancehall-girl costume in opposite colors. Where the staff had red corsets and black skirts, Audrey's corset was black, her skirt red. "I don't guess any of you are really listening to my instructions, are you? Just do your best and watch for your cue to dance. I'll be there to help anyone who starts feeling overwhelmed."

"Are you dancing tonight, Audrey?" Lacey asked.

"No, ma'am." Audrey shook her head. "I hung up my dancin' shoes when I bought this dump."

"That's a shame. I've seen you dance and you're one of the best. You even make me hot." Lacey lifted the hem of her shiny black dancehall-girl skirt and tucked a couple dollar bills under the edge of her red lace, thong under-wear, making certain the greenbacks showed when she moved.

"Lacey, honey, what are you doing?" Bella asked.

"Priming the pump, baby. Priming the pump." Lacey flipped her skirt and turned, flashing her might-as-well-be-naked behind at the group of woman. "If that doesn't get me some tips, these cowboys are all gay."

"Keep it clean, this isn't stripper night at the Ugly Stick Saloon. We'll have all we can do to keep the drinks flowing and the customers happy."

Greta Sue leaned into the storeroom door. "It's time. You want me to open the doors?"

"You have the extra bouncers in place?"

"Cory and Nick McBride are my backups should I need help." Greta cracked her knuckles loudly. "Not that I ever need help."

"Just the same, being everywhere at once is going to be hard. Jackson will be there as well if you need him to step in and settle an argument." Audrey walked toward Greta and patted the large woman's shoulder. "We just don't want to end up in a brawl like last year. The damage to the place eats away at any profits we hope to gain.

"Yes, ma'am. I'll run a tight ship."

"You do that. In the meantime..." Audrey flung out her arm with a flourish. "Let 'em in."

The other waitresses and Libby, the bartender, hurried out to the barroom floor.

Charli hung back. "Audrey, can I talk to you a minute before we go out?"

Audrey looked back, her brows pinched in a hint of a frown. "Can you make it quick? They'll be pouring in before we get into place."

"It's just that I need your advice."

"About?" Audrey glanced over her shoulder as a loud whoop echoed through the empty saloon, and a flood of men in boots trampled in, filling the tables and chairs.

"Connor."

Audrey's gaze returned to Charli. "What about Connor?"

"I think I love him."

Her boss smiled. "Good, then tell him." She looked back toward the barroom. "I think we'll set a record attendance tonight. If all goes well, I can pay off the second mortgage on this place." Audrey's attention moved back to Charli. "Anything else?"

Charli's hands twisted around and around. "What do I do about Original Sin?"

Audrey's brows rose. "You haven't told Connor about your mystery cowboy?"

"No. Not yet." Charli's eyes filled and her throat tightened. "And they'll both be here tonight."

Audrey's eyes widened. "Both? In my place?"

With a nod, Charli brushed the single tear that escaped the corner of her eye. "What should I do?"

"You have to break it off with one and tell the other." Audrey shook her head. "God, I'm glad I'm not single anymore."

"And to think I was bored here in Temptation." Charli laughed, the sound not even funny to her own ears. "I need some of that boredom right now."

"Audrey?" A tall, dark-skinned, man with midnight black hair slicked back behind a black mask stood in the doorway. In his matching black shirt, slacks and cowboy boots, his head topped by a round-brimmed black hat like those worn by Mexican *cabellero's*, Jackson Gray Wolf looked like a throw-back to old Zorro movies still showing at the tiny hours of the morning in black and white. The Kiowa Indian stepped into the doorway of the storeroom. "Libby needs another box of Jack Daniels. They're going to go through a lot tonight."

Audrey leaned up on her toes and pressed a kiss to Jackson's lips. "Thanks for helping."

He caught her around the waist and dragged her close, deepening the kiss. "Wouldn't have missed it for the world," he said, his words muffled by her mouth.

Charli eased past the constricted doorway, leaving Jackson and Audrey alone to their pre-ball groping. With a sigh, Charli trudged toward the barroom, wishing this night was over and that everything had already worked out. As she stepped from behind the bar, Charli's heart cart-wheeled. She braced herself for the onslaught of orders and the requirement to be prepared to flip a bottle or two to entertain the crowd. Slapping away wandering hands of drunken cowboys trying to feel her up, high on booze and adrenaline from their events at the rodeo, seemed the least of her worries tonight.

With her gaze zipping left and right and constantly

turning to see who came through the door, Charli spilled drinks, dropped bottles and tripped, landing in one toothless Mexican's lap to his utter surprise and delight.

When she tried to get up, he refused to let go, pressing his fingers into her sides so hard, she was sure there'd be bruises left behind. Nick McBride, Greta Sue's backup, spun Charli out of the man's grip and onto the dance floor in time for the traditional Party Mixer Dance.

The master of ceremonies Audrey hired for the evening took the microphone at center stage and shouted. "Grab your partner, but don't get too comfortable!" Thirty seconds later, he called out, "Switch!"

Audrey encouraged the waitresses to take a turn around the floor. With a men to women ratio of five-to-one during rodeo weekend, the waitresses helped to even the odds or at least give the men a chance to dance at least once.

Charli spun from one man's arms to the next, her head spinning, her gaze trying to lock onto the men's faces, searching for Connor Mason's blue gray eyes behind the masks. On her third pass from arms to arms, she ended up in the embrace of a man wearing all black like Jackson, only pinned to his jacket was a soft yellow rose.

He leaned down and whispered in her ear. "Love you…naked."

With a gasp, Charli glanced up.

"Switch!"

With a deft move, her partner spun her around and into another man's arms. This cowboy had on the normal jeans and stiffly ironed white shirt of any of the regulars who showed up at the Ugly Stick Saloon on a regular basis. His cowboy boots were worn from use, but polished to a shine. He wore the black mask offered at the door for those who didn't have a costume but wanted to participate in the masquerade.

Noting nothing special about him, Charli craned her neck to see where the man in black with the yellow rose had gone. As her dance partner two-stepped his way around the large oval dance floor, Charli panned the crowd, dread building with each step. She had to find Original Sin, break it off and then find Connor and tell him about her affair with the stranger before someone else had the chance to break the news.

The master of ceremonies called out, "Change partners!"

Charli braced herself, hoping to duck off the dance floor and get back to work.

Instead, the cowboy holding her spun her out, right into another man's arms. She looked up at her new partner, a man dressed all in black, wearing the Zorro-style mask and sporting a yellow rose on his lapel. He smiled a secret smile and pulled her hard against his chest.

Her heart ricocheting off her ribs, Charli opened her mouth to tell him she couldn't see him anymore. Instead, the beat of the music kicked into high gear and the mystery cowboy took off, twirling her under his arm and back into his chest. Every time she tried to say something, he twirled her out again, until the M.C. shouted for the couples to switch partners again.

"No, wait," Charli cried, her voice drowned out by the raucous hoots of the cowboys whose boots pounded the floor.

As the endless song continued, she was practically tossed from one man to another. And soon she was seeing more than one man in black with the yellow rose on his lapel. She blinked. Maybe she was dizzy from all the hand-offs and twirls. Surely there wasn't more than one Zorro with a yellow rose.

Then one passed her on the dance floor. Before he got three steps ahead, another passed her with an identical outfit and a yellow rose. Just in case she thought it was all a hoax, the man winked and grinned.

Charli's knees buckled in the middle of a spin. Her partner caught her before she fell and was trampled by the crowd partaking in the merriment. "Are you okay?"

"No." Charli shook her head. "I need to get back to work. Do you mind?"

He eased her to the side and escorted her off the floor, thanking her for the dance.

She headed back in the direction of her tables, keeping a look out for the mystery Zorros. Now that she wasn't dancing, she didn't see even one. What was up with that?

Any chance at a relationship with the handsome, gentle Connor Mason rode on Charli's ability to wrap up this mess tonight. The sooner the better. Unfortunately, she was there to work and her tables were yammering for drinks.

Begging off the dance floor, Charli hurried back to her coverage area, snatching up empty mugs and bottles, taking orders for more drinks and munchies. By the time she reached the bar, she felt as if she'd run the gauntlet and only thirty minutes of the night had passed. She had another four hours to go.

For the next hour, she worked filling orders, fending off advances and forcing a smile to her face when all she wanted was to scream and run from the bar. The condoms and lubricating jelly slipped to the very back of her mind as she worried about the confrontation ahead when she had to let Original Sin go and tell Connor of her transgressions.

Never mind the package Connor had picked up at the

jewelry store. God forbid he actually planned to propose tonight—in this madhouse, with all these people around. Charli prayed he didn't. Their relationship was too new. Too fresh, too uncertain, even though she knew Connor Mason was a keeper, she needed more time to make up her mind.

"It's your turn. Go on break." Audrey took the tray of empty mugs and bottles from Charli's hands. "Go rest. It's going to be a long night and the show starts soon."

Charli smiled at Audrey and slid behind the bar where she filled a clean mug half-full of ginger ale and hightailed it for the storeroom where she planned to sit on a stack of boxes with her feet up for the few brief minutes she had to herself.

Jackson was leaving the storeroom with a case of vodka on his shoulder, headed toward Libby and the bar. "It's all yours. I snagged a chair from the floor for you girls to use during break."

"Thanks." Charli entered the storeroom and closed the door behind her, reveling in the relative silence. Boxes of wine, cases of beer and staple foods stacked from floor to ceiling along the walls acted as additional insulation against the steady thrum of the country western band, whose speakers blared full blast in order to be heard over the shouts of the patrons of the Ugly Stick Saloon.

Ears ringing, her feet throbbing in the stiletto heels she'd worn with her costume, Charli rounded a tall stack of corn chips to find the wooden chair Jackson commandeered from the overcrowded saloon. The column of chips acted as a wall, blocking the view of the door, making the room seem even more isolated from the hubbub. Charli sank into the chair and let the stress and strain of the evening leach out of her system.

The door to the storeroom opened.

Too tired to get up, Charli leaned back her head. "You can have the chair after my break, but right now, I couldn't move if the building was on fire."

"Poor Charli," a deep, resonant voice preceded the man it belonged to around the stand of nacho chips.

Charli jerked upright, all fatigue fading in a flash as the man in the black suit with the yellow rose stepped into view, the black cloth mask still in place, hiding his face from view. "You."

A smile quirked on the corners of his lips as he plucked the rose from his lapel and drew it down over her eyelids and across her lips.

Charli closed her eyes, her heart skipping several beats, breathing lodging in her throat as she sat frozen to her seat, unable to move or protest the tender assault.

"We've missed you," he whispered.

CHAPTER SIXTEEN

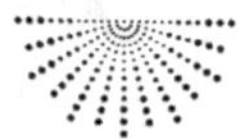

*H*er mouth opened on a gasp and he claimed her lips. Eyes wide now, Charli pulled back, her gaze rising over the stranger's shoulder to see three other men, all identically dressed, each sporting a yellow rose on his lapel. One by one, the men paraded in front of her, trailing their rose across her cheek, her neck, her shoulder.

When they stepped back, Original Sin trailed his rose across the tops of her breasts. "Did you miss us?"

Fully prepared to say no, Charli's mouth opened and nothing came out. She knew Connor was the sure thing, the man a woman could bet her life on—a man a woman could count on to love, honor and commit. Whereas, the men standing in front of her, looking so incredibly sexy, made her so hot with the possibilities, she couldn't work words past her throat.

"I'll take that as a yes." He held out his hand.

Charli placed hers in his and allowed him to pull her to her feet and into his arms.

"I've longed to hold you, to kiss you and to witness the ecstasy in your face as we make love to you."

She swallowed hard, pushing words past her constricted throat. "All of you?"

He smiled. "All of us."

"I'm only on break for fifteen minutes." She glanced at the watch on her wrist. "Make that ten."

A low chuckle rumbled in his chest, reverberating through hers. "What more do we need?" He lifted her skirt, his hands sliding beneath to cup her ass.

In the back of her mind, Charli knew this was all wrong. Connor would never understand. Any relationship she'd hoped to have with him would be beyond repair if she let Original Sin do all the naughty things his gaze told her he would do in just under ten minutes.

No matter how wrong, Charli couldn't say no, couldn't tell him and his buddies to take a hike, couldn't resist the lure of all four men making love to her in the storeroom, fast and furious.

"What if someone enters?" she asked.

"The door's locked." He lifted her legs to wrap around his waist and he nodded at the man who'd moved behind her. "Unlace her."

"Do you know how hard it is to get into this thing?" Was that really her breathless voice? She should be telling these men to leave, not arguing about how difficult it would be to get dressed in the limited amount of time.

With four tall, handsome men filling what little empty space was available in the storeroom, Charli barely had air to breathe.

Then Original Sin slid a finger past the thong of her panties and into her creaming pussy and that's all it took.

Charli's sex drive shot from nil to max in a nano-second, her resistance flying out the door. She tightened her legs around Original Sin's waist and clung as his fingers thrust into her again and again. Then he eased her away from his body.

Two of the men slid alongside Charli ducking beneath her arms, each taking a thigh to spread her legs.

Original Sin tapped her clit with the juices he'd acquired from his foray into her vagina, smearing the liquid over her bud, stroking in long languid strokes.

"Faster."

"Say please."

"Faster, please, damn it," she said through gritted teeth.

His finger paused. "You're a wild and wicked lover, Charli, worthy of many long, hot nights in bed."

Charli bucked, arching toward that magic finger. "Don't tease me. I'm so close."

He stroked her again, drawing all the sensations to the very tip of her clit, then leaving her hanging, high and unsatisfyingly dry.

"You're kidding, right?" With her skirt hiked up around her waist, her corset hanging down so that her boobs bobbed free, she couldn't imagine how it would look if Audrey were to walk in at that moment. And frankly she didn't give a rat's ass if anyone came in, as long as her mystery lover finished what he'd started before she exploded from need.

"Oh, please," she wailed, sure her voice carried over the band's tune in the next room.

With deft fingers, the mystery man slid down the zipper of his trousers, his cock springing free. He held out his hand and the man standing at his side slapped a foil packet into his palm.

"Oh, thank God." At least he'd been foresighted enough to know they needed protection.

Original Sin ripped open the packet and slid the rubber

over his engorged cock. Then he nodded to the man who hadn't touched her at all. "Now, you."

The man smiled. "Are you sure?"

"She won't want to miss this."

Charli's eyes widened, her heart thundering in beat with the lively polka in the saloon. "What won't I want to miss?"

The man beside Original Sin slid his dick out of his trousers, cloaked it in a condom and maneuvered around to the other side of the men holding Charli's thighs. His hands smoothed over her butt cheeks, his fingers seeking the crease between and the tight round hole of her anus.

Her butt muscles clenched in anticipation of what he was about to do. "We only have five minutes leeeeeffft," her voice rose as the man behind her poked his cock into her anus. "Oh, dear. Oh, dear." Charli took swift, shallow breaths, bracing herself as O.S. closed the distance between them, pressing his member to the mound of curls at the apex of her thighs.

The men holding her legs, stood straight and strong, each allowing a hand to rove over her naked breasts, tweaking a turgid nipple.

O.S. leaned against her, his lips teasing her earlobe. "Did I tell you, I love you naked?"

"Yes," she whispered.

Her mystery cowboy touched his cock to her entrance. "Beg for it."

"Please come into me now?"

"No regrets?"

"Oh, God, no! I'm begging you, please. There isn't much time."

Her sexy Zorro wrapped strong hands around her hips and slid into her hot, wet channel. With a man on each side, one behind her pressing into her anus and O.S. in front,

Charli was surrounded by strong, sexy men and completely without a coherent thought in her head besides that of fucking each and every one of them. "Hurry," she urged. She clenched her legs around Original Sin's waist, her ankles locking behind him, forcing him deeper. The two cocks inside her fit so tightly, she couldn't think, couldn't focus—all she could do was feel.

Original Sin thrust in and out, again and again, hard, fast and determined.

Charli clung to him, the hands on her thighs and breasts reminding her there were four men making love to her, not just one, and holy crap, if it felt good.

The pace increased until O.S. jacked in and out of her like a car piston.

Her body on fire, the sensations tumbling one over the other shot Charli into orgasm so intense, she screamed, her fingernails digging into her mystery cowboy's suit jacket.

He thrust one last time, sinking as deep as he could go.

The man behind her pushed deeper as well.

Her breath caught and held, the exquisite pain echoing throughout her body as her Original Sin's cock throbbed within, while the other stranger behind her slid free, releasing the intense pressure.

O.S. brushed a kiss to Charli's lips and lifted her off him, sitting her on a stack of boxes.

For a long moment, she sat in a daze, her heartbeat racing, her pussy and anus tingling from the sweet, sweet torture. Then her world crashed in, reminding her where she was and that she wasn't supposed to be making love in the storeroom, especially with her mystery cowboy.

All the wind left her lungs as she pictured Connor, lying on her bed last night, telling her that he was a one-woman-man. "I can't believe I did this. I can't believe I let it happen again."

Original Sin zipped and buttoned his trousers, then reached out and caressed Charli's cheek. "You are an amazing woman."

"I'm a terrible person," she moaned, burying her face in her hands.

"Should we dress her?" one of the men asked.

"No, let me." Her mystery lover moved behind Charli where she hunched over, wallowing in her horror at having succumbed yet again to the excitement and lust of multiple strangers making love to her. The man's hands moved swiftly and surely, lacing the strings of her corset, pushing her breasts up and out. When he'd finished, he brushed her hair to the side and planted a kiss on her shoulder. "One minute to spare."

"Please leave," she whispered.

"Have we displeased you?"

"Far from it. You all were incredible." She sighed but kept her face buried. "I'm the one who failed."

"Not in our minds." He tugged her off the boxes and into his arms. "You could never disappoint."

"Maybe not you."

"Do you have another lover?"

She laughed, the sound closer to a sob. "Not anymore." She tossed her hair and pushed against his chest. "Go."

"As you wish." He nodded to the other three men, who rounded the column of chip boxes and exited the storeroom, shutting the door. O.S. faced Charli, lifting her hand to his lips. "Until next time."

"No." Charli touched the gorgeous cowboy's arm. "I can't see you again. Any of you."

"Are you certain?" O.S. cupped her chin, staring down into her eyes.

"I can't."

"Ah, there is someone else."

She shook her head, her chest squeezing so tight she could barely breathe. "Not after I confess my sins. You being the biggest sin of all."

A grin spread across his face. "I'm a sin? I'll take that as a compliment." He kissed her again. "I promise that you will figure this all out and that I will see you again. We were meant to be together."

Before Charli could protest further, her mystery cowboy walked out of the storeroom, the music swelled and quelled as the door opened and closed.

For several long moments, Charli stood with a hand pressed to her breaking heart. The tryst in the storeroom with the dark strangers had been incredibly erotic, a total mind-blowing sexual encounter. Charli had been powerless to resist.

Which told her what she should have known from the beginning—she wasn't a one-man-woman. She craved excitement in her sex-life. If the past fifteen minutes was anything to go by, she'd never be true to one without thinking of what the experience was like with four.

Knowing what she had to do, Charli adjusted her skirt, checked her corset to make sure everything was where it should be and sufficiently covered. Then she trudged out of the storeroom into the saloon, ready to find Connor and set the record straight, no matter what it cost.

As she emerged into the ear-numbing din of loud music and cowboys hooting and hollering, her boss caught her arm and swung her toward the bar. "Oh, good, there you are. Time for the show."

Charli planted her heels. "I can't."

"What do you mean you can't? You have to. The men are expecting it, and you're our only singer."

"I need to find Connor."

"It can wait until after the show."

"No, it can't." Though Charli tried to argue, Audrey was already two steps ahead, dragging her behind.

Someone jammed a microphone into Charli's hands and the band struck up the lead-in music. Jackson Gray Wolf grabbed her around the middle and lifted her up onto the bar where Lacey, Kendall, Bella and Libby waited, dressed like Charli in their matching red corsets and black ruffled skirts. With the weight of her transgressions on her shoulders, Charli choked on the first words of the song. Heart pounding, her gaze panned the crowd, searching for Connor's open, honest face, half-afraid she'd find it…even more fearful she wouldn't.

Lacey danced over to where Charli leaned against a support column. "What's wrong with you? The natives are getting impatient. Sing, girl, sing!"

As the band got into the spirit of the bump and grind music, Charli shook off her morose musings and threw her voice into the song, making it as sexy and raunchy as the throng expected and deserved.

The overwhelming majority of the crowd was randy cowboys, liquored up and excited from the adrenalin-kick of riding the rodeo. As the girls danced, the crowd of masked men surged toward the bar, some reaching out to touch.

Jackson stood at the front, warning the men as best he could over the roar of the music and hollering, but they weren't listening.

One man grabbed Libby's ankle and tried to yank her off the bar.

A shout rose from the back of the room.

Charli recognized Mark and Luke Gray Wolf attempting to swim through the crush to get to the bar.

Resident bartender and tough-as-nails biker-babe Libby had it under control. She pressed her free stiletto to the cowboy's forehead and pushed, sending him flying back into the crowd of rabble-rousers.

A cheer went up at the same time as a scream rent the air.

As if in a surreal dream, Charli sang on, as a fight broke out in the middle of the crush, the Gray Wolf twins at the center.

In the sea of faces and cowboy hats, with fists swinging, loud curses flying and men stumbling into one another, one face stood out.

Connor Mason stood to the side of the melee, dressed in a white shirt, white cowboy hat and pulling a white mask from his face, looking every bit the knight in shining armor, come to rescue her from the storm. He glanced around, ducking to avoid a meaty paw of a fist and stared up at Charli, with a grin.

Charli's heart fluttered, her chest tightening until she could barely breathe.

Connor was the man of every woman's dreams, the sweetest, kindest, most predictable man she could ever hope to spend the rest of her life with. Why did she have to go and make love to the men in the storeroom? All for a little short-lived excitement.

Singing from rote memory, Charli's words choked on a sob. And how could she let Connor go? She'd have no other choice, because as soon as she told him what she'd done, he'd walk away, never to again grace her bed.

She'd have to get a new set of batteries for her vibrator. More than that, she'd miss Connor's smile and having someone around to talk to, to sleep with and hold her through the night.

Control disintegrated and the room became a free-for-all brawl.

Sheriff's deputies pushed into the back of the room, one carrying a megaphone. He raised it to speak, but another man in a black business suit, wearing mirrored sunglasses, yanked the device from the deputy's fingers and handed it to the man in the gray business suit beside him. The businessman pointed it toward the bar and yelled, "Elizabeth Stratton, get down off that bar!"

Beside her, Libby, the tough-as-nails, biker-babe bartender turned white and toppled into the crowd of cowboys out cold.

Her head spinning, her pulse hammering against her ears, Charli stared at the mayhem, the man with the megaphone and the jumble of bodies toppling one at a time. Her voice trailed off with the band as she struggled to find Connor's beautiful, sexy face in the horde. Just as she did, a huge cowboy with the build of a professional linebacker powered a left hook into Connor's jaw, sending him breaking through a cluster of men wrestling over a tabletop.

Charli gasped, taking a step toward the edge of the bar. "Connor!"

Another cowboy jerked Connor up by the collar and swung.

Connor ducked his head to the side and the man behind him took the full brunt of the blow, bellowing like a poked bull. He shoved Connor around, balled his fists and landed an upper cut to Connor's belly so fast, Connor, who was still twisted in his shirt from the other guy, couldn't react.

"You bastard!" Charli yelled, then screamed like an Indian on the warpath and launched herself off the corner of the bar and into the fray. She landed on top of the man attacking Connor, rocketing him into another's gut.

Apparently the guy whose back she rode had a girlfriend who was quick to jealousy.

Before Charli could get her own legs under herself, the bleach-blond cowgirl shrieked and grabbed Charli's hair, flinging her around and away from Connor, screaming, "You bitch! Get off my man."

Caught off balance, Charli fell face-first on the floor, the wind knocked out of her lungs.

"Leave my man alone!" Blondie landed in the middle of her back, yanking and tugging at Charli's hair, slapping her upside the head several times, making Charli's ears ring.

When she finally sucked in enough air to make a difference, Charli had just about had enough. She bucked once.

The skinny-ass bitch on top rode her like a mechanical bull.

Well, ride this.

Anger spiked and adrenaline kicked in, giving Charli enough oomph, she bucked and rolled, twisting the vicious bitch over onto her back. She straddled her and pinned her arms above her head. "Don't call me a bitch and leave me the fuck alone!" She wanted to, but she didn't, slap the woman, although it took all her control not to.

Before Charli could rise and put distance between herself and the crazy woman, men formed a circle around the women on the floor, shouting, "Cat fight!" The circle grew, hoots and hollering going up all around, drawing more spectators.

"Sorry, fellas, this one's over." Charli stood and reached down a hand to help the blonde up.

The woman clasped Charli's hand and shot to her feet,

her lips pulled back into a sneer as she yanked Charli forward and slammed a fist into her belly. "Not yet, it ain't."

Doubled over, her hands clutching her belly, Charli gasped. "Oh, you did not just do that."

Blondie stood with her fists on her hips. "I sure did and I'm gonna do it again."

Her lips forming a thin line, Charli forced her back straight, despite the pain in her midsection. "Not in this lifetime."

The other woman took a swing. Charli leaned to the side just enough the woman's arm sailed past her, her momentum carrying her forward. Charli stuck out her foot, pressed a hand to the woman's shoulder and sent her flying into the arms of the men around her. "Don't fuck with me."

The woman screeched like a wounded cat and spun to face Charli. "You want some of this?" She wiggled her fingers, urging Charli forward. "Come on."

All Charli wanted was to get to where Connor was and make sure he was okay, not lying comatose under a table. "I don't have time for this."

When the woman came at her again, Charli braced herself, and waited until the last minute, then ducked to the right, raising her knee to Blondie's belly, landing it hard in her breadbasket.

The woman collapsed to the floor on her hands and knees, coughing.

One end of the circle of men broke open and a deputy sheriff shouldered his way into the middle. "What's going on here?"

The man Charli had landed on pointed. "That bitch attacked me and then she tried to kill my girlfriend."

Without waiting to hear Charli's side of the story, the deputy snapped a cuff to her wrist. "You're coming with me."

CHAPTER SEVENTEEN

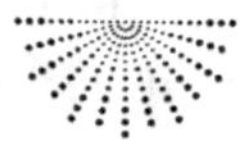

"**T**hat man's lying," Charli cried out, but her voice was lost in the cursing and yelling going on all around. She yanked away from the deputy, determined to find Connor.

"Sorry, lady, but you have to come with me." The deputy dragged her toward the front door.

"No, I need to check on Connor. That baboon could have killed him. He could be lying under a table dying. Let me go!"

As she kicked, scratched and clawed her way toward Connor, the deputy lost patience and slung her over his shoulder, pushing his way through the thinning crowd near the front entrance. Once outside, he dumped her into the back of his SUV, clipped the other end of the cuff to the wire mesh separating the front of the vehicle from the back.

"You can't haul me in. I didn't do anything," she called out.

"Tell it to the judge." He shut the door and left her sitting there and went back inside the saloon. A few minutes later, he returned, leading a big man in a black suit with a bloody nose, his hands zip-tied behind his back. The deputy loaded the man into the other side of the SUV, then slid into the driver seat and drove away from the Ugly Stick Saloon.

"Don't leave! I need to go back in," Charli insisted.

"No can do," Deputy Dense said with a southern drawl.

"But people are getting hurt. I could help."

Sirens screamed past them as more county sheriff cars and the local volunteer fire department arrived with the Emergency Medical Technicians and ambulances.

"Let the professionals handle it."

"But—" She pulled against the manacle on her wrist.

"Not listening."

Charli sat in the back next to the big guy with the bloody nose, who didn't fit into the usual crowd at the Ugly Stick Saloon. "Who are you?"

He stared straight ahead, without answering.

"I get it. You're one of the strong silent types." She huffed. "Good, didn't wanna talk anyway." She twisted around trying to look over her shoulder as the SUV pulled off the short road to the saloon onto the highway. "Where are you taking us?"

"To Hole In The Wall. The jail in Temptation is going to be too full to handle everyone."

Red, blue and yellow lights flashed, strobing the night with color all around the saloon. "You wouldn't have to fill up the jails if you'd just let us go."

Charli was ignored again, by both the deputy driver and the man sitting beside her, blood drying on his lip.

As the colored lights faded, all Charli could see was the big Texas night sky filled to overflowing with bright, beautiful stars. Her vision blurred with a wash of tears. "I never got to tell him." She sighed. "It's just as well. He wouldn't understand." She snorted softly, leaning her head onto her arms. "I don't even understand."

Her silent seat partner harrumphed, the first sound he'd made since he'd been shoved into the back of the SUV.

Charli tipped her head on her arms and stared across at him. "What would you do, if you thought you were in love with someone, but that you might also be in love with another?"

The big guy's gaze shifted toward her for a nanosecond, then back to the front again.

Charli sighed again. "I know, it all sounds wishy-washy, but they both have great qualities. On the one hand, Original Sin knows exactly what buttons to push to make me so hot, I swear my hair lights on fire."

Those dark eyes shifted toward her. "T.M.I.," he muttered.

"Ah, so you do have a voice." Charli sat up straight. "You're a man, answer this—"

"No." He cut her off before she got any farther. "I don't get involved when it's not my business. And you, little lady, are not my business."

Her brows rose. "Just what is your business?"

"I'm a bodyguard."

Charli's brows rose further, a smile lifting the corners of her lips. "Did you lose something?"

His brows furrowed. "I shouldn't be here. I didn't throw the first punch. I was only protecting my boss."

"Yeah, yeah. Another sob story." The deputy glanced in the rearview mirror. "Cry to the judge."

"He's not very sympathetic, is he?" Charli stuck out her tongue at the back of the deputy's head.

"I saw that."

"So what are you going to do, arrest me?" Charli chuckled and turned back to the bodyguard. "Anyway, what would you do if you fancied yourself in love with two people? One the exciting, blood-stirring spontaneous type and the other, the steady, you-can-bank-your-life-on-me type? Which would you choose?"

"Not that it's my business, but the bank." The deputy shot a glance at Charli in the mirror. "Likely he won't spend his nights carousing in a bar, picking fights."

The bodyguard shook his head. "Nah, she should choose the exciting, spontaneous one. Life's too short to end up bored out of your mind."

Charli stared from the deputy to the bodyguard and back. "You two are not helping. I have to decide, tonight."

"It all boils down to what you want out of life," the body-guard stated.

"Sadly, I want both." But that wasn't the option she had to choose from. And given that by choosing one, she'd be sealing her fate with the other. Most likely, she'd end up with neither. Charli laid her face on her arms, knowing she had to get this matter settled and soon—she wouldn't sleep until she did. The guilt and turmoil ate at her gut, twisting her insides into knots.

When they arrived at the jail in Hole In The Wall, Charli asked to use the phone. Her first and only call was to Audrey, the one person in all her world she could count on to bail her out. She tried the phone at the Ugly Stick Saloon. No answer. Then she tried Audrey's cell phone, which rang four times then went to voicemail. Charli left a message and handed the phone to the bodyguard. So much for being bailed out anytime soon. Hopefully, Audrey would sort quickly through the disaster of the evening, the sheriff's deputies and wreckage of the saloon.

Charli cringed at what she'd find the next day when she returned with the rest of the staff to set everything to rights before the next wave of rodeo contestants and locals arrived that evening. Assuming she was sprung from jail by then.

Focusing on the mess of the saloon helped her to push the main source of her worries to the back of her mind, if only for a moment.

The deputy led her to an empty jail cell and locked the bars behind her. "The judge is on his way in to set bail. Shouldn't be long."

"Good, I have a lot to do before this night is over." She sat on the inch-thick mattress on the single bunk and stared at the empty cell across from hers, silently rehearsing the speech she'd give Connor when she finally saw him. And no matter what, she'd see him as soon as she was released from this hell hole.

Another deputy appeared, leading the bodyguard. He opened the door to the larger cell across from her and motioned for him to enter. The man sat on a hard bench and leaned back against the wall, his hands clasped between his knees. "I didn't sign on for this."

"Yeah, you and me both." Charli smiled across the space between their cells. "Since we're going to be neighbors, what's your name?"

"Race Bennett."

"I'm Charli Sutton." She smiled. "Nice to meet you."

He nodded. "Same."

Charli clapped her hands on her bare knees, the ruffles of her skirt sliding to either side. "So, Race, who's your boss?"

"James Stratton, of the Manhattan Stratton dynasty."

The name rang a bell, but Charli couldn't quite put her finger on it. "Should I know him?"

"He's one of the wealthiest men in the United States."

Flashes of news reports zipped through Charli's head. "That Stratton?"

The bodyguard nodded. "The one and only."

"What the hell was he doing at the Ugly Stick Saloon? Aren't there classier joints for him to hang at?"

A smirk twisted the bodyguard's mouth. "Looking for his daughter."

The bar scene flashed in her mind and Charli's brows furrowed. "Oh, that would be the guy with the megaphone, yelling for Elizabeth somebody-or-other."

"Stratton," the bodyguard corrected.

"Didn't she disappear a couple years back? I thought she was dead."

"He won't give up as long as there's not a body."

"Did he find her at the Ugly Stick?" Charli couldn't imagine finding anyone that important at the saloon.

"He's convinced he did. I'm not so sure."

"Well, good luck to him." Charli glanced up as another deputy led a procession down the narrow aisle between the jail cells. Behind him, three men in black suits marched in sync.

When the deputy paused to open the door to the same cell in which the bodyguard sat, he moved to the side, giving Charli a clear view of the men.

The air left her lungs in a whoosh and she nearly fell out of her seat. All three men wore identical black suits and sported yellow roses on their lapels, their masks removed, their faces bare, uncovered and clear to see. "You," she rasped.

On his way through the open cell door, the lead man paused, his face flushing crimson.

The other two men pushed past him into the cell, all looking so similar to the first, they had to be related.

All the blood rushed from her head down to her gut as Charli rose from her seat on the bed and stalked to the bars, her fingers gripping the rungs. "Oh, my god, you're the ones."

The man at the back of the line frowned, his head dipping low, his gaze going anywhere but toward hers. "Don't know what you're talking about, ma'am." The way the tips of his ears turned a ruddy red gave away his lie.

"The hell you don't." She leaned forward, her cheeks pressing against the bars. "You're the men who've been in on the dirty tricks."

Not one of the men acknowledged or denied her statement, adding credence to her accusation.

Charli studied them, her eyes narrowed. "I know you, don't I?"

The one closest to her smiled. "Maybe."

"You're the O'Briens." She pointed to the first one. "You're Gabe, Tanner, and Sean. I know your sister, Molly, she applied to the Ugly Stick just last week." Her face heated as she asked, "Which one of you was the first…my original sin? The one who showed up at Judge Stephens's pool that night over two weeks ago?" She cast a glance at Race, wishing she could conduct this inquisition out of his presence.

The three men looked from one to the other and finally, the one called Gabe shrugged. "We have no idea what you're talking about." This time, they all glanced at her, with open, blank gazes.

If they were lying, they'd figured out how in the past minute, which led Charli to believe they were telling the truth for the first time.

"Where's the fourth guy? Is he another of your brothers? Aren't there four O'Brien men?" Leaning into the bars, Charli felt as if she was the closest to learning the truth than she'd ever been.

"Sorry, our youngest brother moved to NYC a couple months ago."

Charli's heart sank and her grip tightened on the bars, her

lifeline in the sea of disappointment. "Then who is he? Who's the other man in the foursome?" She stared at each man, moving her gaze down the line.

All three men clamped their lips tight. "Sorry. It's not our place to tell."

Her jaw slackened, her anger rising. "Are you kidding me?"

The bodyguard who'd been sitting silently on the bench behind them stood. "Tell the lady what she wants to know."

"Or what?" Gabe O'Brien asked. "You'll take on all three of us?"

"Bring it." Sean and Tanner shucked their jackets, exposing broad shoulders and trim waists.

"Not worth it, Race." Charli leaned against the rails. "They're not gonna tell and you'll only get slapped with more jail-time. I'm not worried about it. As far as I'm concerned, I'm done with them. All of them. I've had enough lying and secrets to last a lifetime."

The brothers all looked at her at once. "Don't give up now. It's just starting to get interesting."

"Yeah, well, I'm done with the three of you. It'll be hard enough seeing you guys on the street, knowing what you know about me." Heat filled her chest and rose up to burn in her cheeks. Charli sank onto the bed. "Just do me a favor, will ya, and keep it to yourselves. Promise me, or I'll sic Race on you after all."

The three O'Briens raised their hands and Gabe spoke for them. "We don't kiss and tell."

"Uh-huh." Charli laughed, the effort completely without humor. "I'm supposed to believe that?"

"An O'Brien's word is his bond."

"Well, good, at least there's that." Charli leaned back

against the wall, closing her eyes. "How did my life get to be such a big damn mess?"

"Maybe I can help you out." A warm, sexy voice sounded from the hallway leading into the cell area.

Charli's eyes flicked open. For a second, she thought the fourth man in the crew had arrived. But when she opened her eyes, her stomach did a back-flip to a belly-flop.

Connor Mason stood outside her cell, dressed in his white shirt, carrying his white cowboy hat and sporting a dark purple shiner on his left eye and a bruise on his chin. He smiled and winced. "Hey, beautiful."

A sheriff's deputy reached around Connor to unlock the door to Charli's cell. "You're free to go. You can thank Mr. Mason for posting the bail."

"Thanks, Jack." Connor shook hands with the deputy. "See you at the rodeo tomorrow?"

"Wouldn't miss it. Could use a little rest and relaxation after tonight's haul."

Connor held out his hand to Charli. "Come on, I'll take you home."

Charli glanced across the aisle at the men behind the bars in the other cell, her stomach a mass of butterflies, just waiting for the O'Briens to spill the beans and confess their part in the whole mystery cowboy charade.

They nodded toward Connor as one.

"Hey, Connor," Gabe said. "Surprised you made it out on your own two feet."

"I would have been on the other side of the bars had someone not cleaned my clock. The EMTs found me out cold under a table."

"Oh, baby." Charli hurried forward, glaring at the deputy. "I was trying to get to you, but some witch decided it was time for a girl fight."

"I heard." Connor grinned and pulled her into his arms, brushing a kiss across her lips. "Quite the talk, how you showed her."

Charli's lips thinned. "Stupid woman. I wasn't there to fight." She dragged in a long breath. "I wanted to talk to you."

"Same here. And I didn't get that dance you promised."

"Hey, what about us?" Sean O'Brien called out.

Connor grinned at the men. "Molly's signing for the three of you now. Won't be but another minute or so.

The door to the outer offices opened and the perky auburn-haired baby sister of the O'Brien brothers bounced through. "Caused enough trouble for one night, boys?"

Charli paused in front of the bodyguard. "Need me to bail you out?"

He shook his head. "My partner or my boss will be by soon enough. Don't worry about me. You have enough to think about." He nodded toward Connor. "If he gives you any trouble, I'll be staying at the Temptation lodge…once I get sprung from this joint. Call me."

Her heart warmed by a stranger, Charli let Connor lead her toward the exit.

Connor waved to the O'Briens. "I'll be at the ranch, bright and early tomorrow morning to help load the horses." He hooked Charli's elbow, escorted her through the doors and out into the night.

As she climbed into the cab of Connor's pickup, Charli's heartbeat ratcheted up into high gear. The time had come to fess up, to set the story straight. She waited until Connor pulled out onto the highway headed for Temptation. "I'm sorry you got hurt in that brawl."

Connor glanced sideways, with a smile. "I just hate that you had to spend time in a jail cell."

Charli shrugged. The experience hadn't been that bad and

she'd at least discovered the identities of three of the four men who'd made love to her in the storeroom earlier that evening. For what it was worth, she had some of the truth. "We need to talk."

"I agree. But can we save it until I get you home? I could use an icepack on this eye, and I'm sure you'll want to clean up and change out of that outfit." He nodded toward the corset and skirt. "Not that I don't like it, but I'm feeling a bit overdressed with you."

"But I wanted to tell you—"

His hand reached out and captured hers. "Let it ride."

The warmth of his calloused fingers seeped into her hand. Charli leaned back against the leather seat, chewing on her bottom lip. Okay, just until she got to her place. She'd enjoy the last few minutes she'd be with Connor, holding his hand as if he might actually be in love with her.

She almost laughed, but she was afraid the laughter would turn hysterical and she'd bust out crying. Why, oh, why had she made love to the men in the storeroom, especially knowing Connor would be there that night and she'd be breaking it to him that she'd had an affair while dating him?

Sitting silently beside him now was tearing her heart in two. This time tomorrow, she'd be alone again, unloved, unwanted and back to square one, only worse. Now she knew how exciting Temptation could be with the right person...or persons. But her adventure would be over and she'd have to move on.

"Tired?" Connor squeezed her hand gently.

"Exhausted." All the worry, the fight, the internal battles had taken their toll. Charli closed her eyes and let the silence wash over her like a soothing balm, the scent of leather and cowboy lulling her into a false sense of calm. Her announcement could wait until she had him alone at her house. For now, she wanted to hold Connor's hand and pretend all was right with the world. Even if only for the few minutes involved in driving from Hole In The Wall to Temptation and her house.

All too soon, Connor pulled into her driveway and released her hand.

Charli sat staring forward, all the dread of the evening welling up inside. The time had come to confess.

Connor shifted into park and dropped down out of the truck, rounding the hood to open her door.

All her energy drained away, Charli let him. After the craziness of the past couple weeks, she'd be glad to put this all behind her and move on with a normal life. She snorted. Who was she kidding? She'd loved almost every minute—except the ones she'd spent worrying about her deception and lies. She'd never felt so alive and desired. And all that would go away once they had their "talk".

"Come here, baby. You look all done in." Connor held out his hands, grabbed her around the waist and swung her down to the ground and into his arms.

She braced her hands on his chest. "Connor—"

Before she could say another word, he kissed her, his mouth sealing over hers, his tongue delving between her teeth to slide alongside hers.

The longer Connor kissed her, the weaker Charli's knees grew until she had to slide her arms around his waist to help hold herself up.

Without breaking their connection, Connor scooped her up into his arms and carried her to her door. His head came up with a butterfly kiss to the tip of Charli's nose. "Where's your key?"

Breathless and a little lightheaded, Charli chuckled. "At the Ugly Stick Saloon in my purse."

"That could be a problem."

With a grin, she nuzzled the side of his neck. "Only if I didn't keep a spare under the flowerpot on the porch."

He set her on her feet.

Charli retrieved the key and handed it to him, her hands shaking enough she feared she'd fumble and drop it.

Connor opened the door.

When Charli tried to step past him to enter, he put out his hand. "Wait."

Then he scooped her into his arms and carried her across the threshold, like a newly married man, carrying his new wife into the home they'd share for the rest of their lives.

A lump the size of her fist lodged in Charli's throat and tears welled in her eyes. She blinked fast, praying Connor didn't see them. It was one thing to blow the relationship of a lifetime, it was another to be caught crying about it when it was your own darned fault.

"Put me down, Connor," Charli choked out, past constricted vocal cords.

"I will." He grinned and marched through the living room to Charli's bedroom. "Now." He set her on her feet and smoothed a hand through her hair. "You are the most beautiful woman I've ever had the pleasure of making love to."

"Connor." She pressed a finger to his lips. "You need to listen to me."

He kissed her finger and drew her hand into his. "Me first." His hands slipped around her waist. "I've had my eye on you since I returned to Temptation and the first time I heard you sigh across the bar in the Ugly Stick Saloon."

"That seems like such a long time ago." Yet the meeting had only been a couple weeks earlier.

"I think it was love at first sight."

Although it hadn't been exactly love at first sight for her, she remembered her initial attraction to the fair-haired ex-marine, his face clearly etched in her mind, his words, challenging her to find the excitement in Temptation. Charli shook her head. "How long had you been deployed?"

"Long enough to know what I wanted when I got back from the sandbox." His fingers twisted the strings on the back of her corset. "And I want you." He tugged the bow, the corset strings loosened and her breasts spilled from their confinement.

"Connor, I—" God, he wasn't making this easy.

"Shh." He pressed his lips to hers. "Just let me love you.

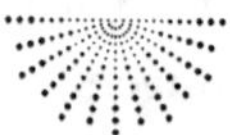

CHAPTER EIGHTEEN

*H*is mouth moved across hers, teasing her lips open so that his tongue could slip between her teeth and claim hers.

The long slow slide of warm wetness made Charli's pussy clench, heating her core. Her fingers threaded through his hair, drawing him closer, her hips pressing into his, her naked breasts rubbing against the crisp white cotton of his button-down shirt.

He found the zipper of her skirt and slid it down, pushing the fabric over her hips. The smooth, silky material floated to the floor, a black pool of ruffles, and she stepped out of the circle. He worked the strings looser on the corset and let it follow the skirt.

When she stood before him in nothing but her black, lace thong panties, all her thoughts of telling him the truth had flown. All her focus turned to getting him as naked as she was. The sooner the better, before her body exploded into a fiery inferno of need.

Charli grabbed his arms and turned him until his back

was to the bed. Then, with a wide smile, she pushed him onto it.

As he fell, he grabbed her around the middle, dragging her down.

She straddled his hips, her pussy grinding against the ridge beneath his fly, an urgent reminder of her near nakedness and his fully clothed body.

Her fingers flew over the buttons on his shirt, ripping them loose of the holes. As she moved down his muscled chest, she opened the shirt, kissing a path that followed her work until she reached the waistband of his jeans. With a sharp tug, she pulled the hem of his shirt out of the band and shoved the edges open.

God, he had a beautiful chest. Tanned, toned and contoured around each muscle from his pecks to his abs. The dark brown nipples nestled in a smattering of manly hairs.

Too aroused to slow her descent, Charli eased off the hard ridge of his cock and stood beside the bed, working the buttoned-fly of his jeans. She struggled with the first, then ripped the remaining open.

His cock jutted out, rising straight to the sky, hot, hard and thick.

Digging her fingers into his waistband, Charli dragged his jeans down to his boots. She grabbed his boot heels and tugged off one, then the other boot, tossing them behind her as she did.

Naked at last, he sat up, his legs falling over the side of the bed. He grabbed her wrists and pulled her into the V between his legs. "What about foreplay?"

"I'm working on that." She dropped to her knees and took his cock in her hands, her fingers kneading his balls, while her tongue touched the tip and slid down his length in one, long, slow movement.

His fingers fisted in her hair, his body tensing. "What about you? Don't you want me to do that to you?"

The guilt she felt reared its ugly head for a second and she almost lost her concentration. But she pushed all thoughts of the past, her indiscretions and her ultimate confession to the back of her mind, focusing on the man, promising to send him away with at least one good memory, before she shattered his trust. "I want this to be all about you." Her mouth closed around his cock as she took him in.

"Umm. That's feels so good." He shook his head, lifting her off his member. "But it can be so much better." He scooted back on the bed until he lay in the middle and dragged her up beside him.

Eager to please him first, Charli leaned across him, taking his cock in her hand, running her fingers down his length.

Connor eased her up onto all fours and ducked his head beneath her, planting her knees on either side of his head. "Now, I can taste you as well."

He urged her to spread her legs wider, dropping her down to within reach of his mouth.

Charli creamed, her pussy throbbing, aching to be fucked. As soon as Connor's tongue touched her clit, she rocketed up the orgasm ladder, shooting for heaven. She sucked Connor's cock deeper into her mouth, taking his full length, all the way to the back of her throat. Her fingers curled around his scrotum, massaging the sacks as he pumped in and out of her mouth.

His tender assault on her pussy had her gasping, her body jerking with each electric thrust of his tongue across the bundle of nerves so tightly coiled. When she burst over the edge, she could bear no more and lifted her bottom up and away from his mouth, her entire body quivering.

Connor flipped her over on her back and dove for his

jeans, returning with a condom, ripping into the package with his teeth. Then he lay between Charli's legs, leaning over her as her spasms began to subside. "Don't stop now." He reached between them and touched her there, igniting a whole new barrage of electric shocks pinging through her body.

Charli wrapped her legs around Connor's waist and pulled him close.

He paused with his cock nudging her entrance, teasing her with the possibilities of his thickness filling her, stretching her channel.

"Don't stop now!" she cried, echoing his sentiment of a moment before.

"I love you, Charli." He drove into her in one long, hard thrust.

Charli's breath caught on a gasp, her heart squeezing so tightly in her chest she was certain she would die right there in Connor's arms, making love to a man she could have spent her life with...had she lived longer.

He pulled out to the very tip of his magnificent cock and thrust again, settling into a rhythm, his speed increasing with the tension in his muscles.

Charli clung to his shoulders, her legs clamped around his middle urging him closer, faster, harder.

On his final thrust, he drove deep, his cock pulsing inside her, his breath caught and held. When at last he relaxed, he dropped to the mattress beside her, gathering her in his arms, holding her against his muscular chest. His breathing evened out and he sighed. "You're incredible, Charli."

Charli reveled in the closeness, inhaling the scent of the man to remember when she slept alone again. She didn't want to break the mood, to ruin the most beautiful love-making she'd ever experienced. For a long time, she lay trying to gather the courage to tell Connor the truth.

"Connor, I need to tell you something," she whispered, half-hoping he wouldn't hear her.

"Ummm," he mumbled. "I haven't been totally up front with you," she said, her voice fading off into the darkness.

"Ummm," he mumbled again.

" Since I started dating you, I've made love to another man, whose name I don't even know." She held her breath waiting for Connor to say something, to pull away, to yell at her...something.

He lay still, his chest rising in a slow, lazy rhythm.

"Aren't you mad?" Her heart hammering against her ribs, Charli leaned up on an elbow and stared down into Connor's face—his relaxed, sleeping face. The man had gone to sleep!

Charli shook her head, staring down at the man she was hopelessly falling in love with. She settled back in the crook of his arm, snuggling close to his naked body, relishing her last night with him and the way he made her feel safe and loved.

Soon, sleep claimed her. Somewhere in the night, she dreamed she was lying with Connor in a field of bluebonnets and Indian paintbrushes, the sun glowing down on them, warming their skin. The warmth faded, a cold wind blowing over her skin. In her dream, Connor had gone, leaving her alone in the field, the sun having set and a starless night closed in around her.

She called out, but he didn't come. Tears slipped from the corners of her eyes, sobs rising in her chest. "Please," she called. "Don't go."

"I'm here," a deep, resonant voice called out. "I'm not leaving. I love you too much...naked."

Something smooth and velvety soft brushed across her lips, over her chin and down her neck.

"Connor?"

"Guess again."

There was that voice again, like melted chocolate, spreading into every pore of her body. "Am I dreaming?" Charli asked.

"A little." He chuckled. "Open your eyes, my beautiful, sexy lover."

The velvety soft thing slid across a breast, tickling her nipple. Fire ignited in her core and Charli blinked open her eyes and stared up into a masked face.

Suddenly awake, her gaze darted to the pillow beside her, where Connor had been sleeping. Hadn't it been only moments before?

"Looking for someone?" Original Sin's lips curled upward while his hand trailed a soft yellow rose lower still across Charli's belly.

Where was Connor? Heart pounding, Charli glanced over O.S.'s shoulder. "How did you get in?"

"I have my ways."

"Well, you have to leave." Nothing would risk what she'd found with Connor.

"So soon? But I've only just arrived."

"I don't care. It's over between you and me. I love Connor."

The eyes behind the mask blinked and the smile twisted. "Does he make you as hot as I do?"

Charli sat up, leaning her back against the headboard, dragging the sheet up over her nakedness. "Hotter."

Perched on the edge of the bed, O.S. dragged the rose over Charli's hand, the one holding the sheet. "Will he share you with others?"

"I don't need others. He's more than enough for me," she declared, surprised at her own words.

"Does he plan dirty tricks to feed your sexual appetite?" His hand descended on her calf, squeezing it gently.

Charli jumped, her foot kicking away from his grip. "Get out," she cried.

The sharp movement caught O.S. unawares and he rolled off the side of the bed, his head connecting with the foot-board, before he landed flat on his back.

He lay still for a long time.

Oh god, what had she done? Charli bunched the sheet around her and peered at the man lying on the floor. "Er...sir? Original Sin? Mister?"

He didn't stir, his eyes closed, the mask askew.

Holy crap, had she killed him?

Easing a foot off the bed, she dropped to the floor and leaned over the man dressed in the black pants, black shirt and black mask. His hat had fallen off and lay on the floor beside him, exposing a shock of sandy blond hair. A strikingly familiar shade of sandy blond.

Charli reached out, grasping the edge of the mask. As she dragged it up over his forehead, a hand snagged her wrist, but he was too late.

"Connor?" Charli stared down at the man who'd kept her guessing for the past two weeks. The mystery man behind the dirty tricks, the mastermind responsible for making her life crazy, hectic, and miserable to the point she thought she'd have to leave town for good. "Bastard!" She jerked her hand, trying to escape his grip. "You bastard." Her voice cracked. "Do you think I'm just some stupid woman you can trick into dirty sex?"

"No, no. Not at all." Connor sat up, hauling her into his arms, refusing to let her go. "I did it all for you."

"What? Made a fool out of me in front of everyone?"

"If you mean in front of the O'Briens, they can be trusted. No one else knows but you and me."

"You lied."

"For you."

"It doesn't change anything. You lied."

"Because I love you." He held both of her wrists in one hand and smoothed the hair from her face with the other. "I didn't want you to leave Temptation. I knew I had to make this town interesting enough to keep you here."

Tears trickled from the corners of Charli's eyes. "You must think I'm the most gullible, stupid woman in the county." She leaned her head against his chest. "How could you?"

"Oh, baby, I only wanted to make you happy. Give you a little excitement to keep you around." His fingers ran along her cheek. "How else could I have the time to really get to know you?"

"You could have done it the normal way. Ask me out on a date."

"You were ready to walk...no run...away from this town. And I'm tired and selfish enough to want to keep you here. Please...don't be mad at me." A hand ran down her back. "I love you, Charli Sutton. Enough to share you with other men, if that's what it takes to make you happy."

Charli held onto her anger, gathering it like a cloak to protect her from what had the potential to scare the crap out of her. "You need to leave."

"Not until you forgive me."

"That might be a very long time."

A grin spread his lips. "Good, then I'll be around for a very long time. I'm not going anywhere until you tell me you forgive me and tell me that you love me."

Her head shook. "But I don't love you."

"That's not what you said a minute ago."

"Oh!" She shoved against his chest, her fingers flattening on his dark shirt. "I should be very angry with you."

He smiled, that charming quirk of his lips that Charli had fallen for the first time she'd seen him.

"But you can't stay mad at me."

"I can."

"Not when I do this." He kissed the tip of her nose. "And this." His free hand tweaked the tip of her nipple.

Despite her determination to resist, Charli's body responded, both nipples drawing into tight little buds. "You don't play fair."

"That's what you like most about my dark side, isn't it?" He caught her bottom lip between his teeth and tugged, letting it go. "Original Sin. Was that what you named me?"

Charli shifted, straddling his hips, glad she was naked and ready to torture the man who'd tortured her for weeks. "I had a hard time distinguishing between the four of you. I couldn't call you Man One and Man Two. And my attention always came back to you, the original." She slid his belt from the belt loops on his jeans, easing it out from under him. "Why did you bother dressing, when you knew you'd end up naked anyway?"

"I thought you might enjoy undressing me as much as I like when you do it." He pulled her close, her wrists trapped between them. "Do you really want me to go? To walk out of your life and leave you alone?" His gaze narrowed, and he sighed. "I'll do it, if that's what you really want."

Charli stared into his gray-blue eyes for a long moment, trying to summon her anger and failing miserably. "I want to be mad at you, but I can't. You're too damned adorable as both yourself and Original Sin."

"Thank God." He let out the breath he'd been holding and

released her hands. "I thought you'd send me packing and I didn't want to go."

Her brows furrowed and she poked a finger into his chest. "Don't think you're getting off easy on this? That's a pretty big lie to carry around. You'll have some major atonement to perform before you're fully forgiven."

"Name my punishment," he said the words, a smile lighting his face.

Her lips twitched and she pushed him back to lie on the floor. "I'll think of some really dirty trick to keep you in line."

"Promises, promises."

"For now, you may kiss me." She leaned toward him, her mouth covering his a tingle of excitement spreading throughout her body at the thought of spending the rest of her life with this man.

Connor's hands slid around her naked waist and down over the curve of her ass. "As you wish."

Make-up sex promised to be oh, so fine...

If you enjoyed this book, try the other books in the
Ugly Stick Saloon Series

Boots & Chaps (#1)
Boots & Sex Ed (#2)
Boots & Leather (#3)
Boots & Promises (#4)
Boots & Bareback (#5)
Boots & Dirty Tricks (#6)
Boots & Lace (#7)
Boots & Roses (#8)
Boots & Buckles (#9)
Boots & the Wishes (#10)

Boots & Twisters (#11)
Boots & the Bachelor (#12)
Boots & the Rogue (#13)
Boots & the Heartbreaker (#14)
Boots & Wings (#15)

BOOTS & LACE

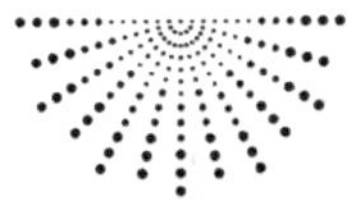

UGLY STICK SALOON SERIES #7

New York Times & *USA Today*
Bestselling Author

ELLE JAMES

writing as

MYLA JACKSON

BOOTS
&
LACE
UGLY STICK SALOON
New York Times Bestselling Author
ELLE JAMES
writing as
MYLA JACKSON

CHAPTER ONE

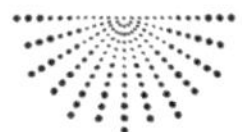

The cowboy at the bar had captured Lacey Lambert's attention from the beginning, with his dark good looks and an expression so somber it made her sad. He sat by himself, head down, staring into his mug of beer.

As Lacey waited tables in the busy Ugly Stick Saloon, her gaze wandered back to him more and more.

Fellow waitress Kendall Mason passed her carrying a tray full of whiskey shooters and beer. "Did you see him?" she whispered.

Lacey, on her way back to the bar with an empty tray, played dumb and asked, "See who?"

Kendall stopped long enough to throw a frown. "Seriously? The smokin' hot cowboy at the bar. You can't miss him."

Lacey Lambert hadn't missed him. In fact she could barely concentrate on her duties with the man sitting in the seat next to where she stopped to place her orders with Libby, the bartender. Every time she pulled up to the bar, her heartbeat fluttered and she forgot how to breathe.

All bad news as far as she was concerned. Flirting, having sex, playing around were all fine in her books, but getting involved? No way.

Lacey shrugged. "So, he's cute."

"Honey, he's not cute, he's…" Kendall fanned her face. "Va-va-va-voom!"

"Now, what would Ed think if he heard you talking like that?"

"He'd know I was only looking out for my best friend. He has nothing to worry about. I'm totally in love with my hunka-hunka-burnin' love."

Lacey shrugged. "So, the cowboy is easy on the eyes. He's probably full of himself." Her ex had been one of those. Easy to look at and easy with the women. Thus the "ex" part to the equation. "I'm not interested."

"Such a shame. I bet he's nice and nicer in bed."

"Not many good-looking guys are nice. And most aren't that great in bed."

Kendall glared at Lacey. "Ed is. And Jackson and Luke and Mark from what Audrey and Libby say—"

Lacey raised her empty hand. "Okay, okay, you've made your point. I don't have time to flirt. I have an order to fill."

"I'll take your tables if you want to work on getting his number."

A cowboy at one of the tables hollered, "Kendall! We gonna get those shooters sometime today?"

"Coming," Kendall called out. To Lacey she said, "Think about it. You could use a man in your life."

"They're only good for one thing."

"Sex?"

"Okay, two." Lacey grinned. "Sex and taking out the trash."

"You're hopeless. What happened to the carefree, happy-go-lucky roommate I knew?"

"You moved out with a gorgeous cowboy." Lacey sighed. "I'm going to miss you."

"Same here."

The customer yelled again. "Kendall!"

"Keep your pants on. I'm coming." Kendall scooted away from Lacey.

Lacey sucked in her breath and proceeded to the bar.

A beautiful woman had planted herself in the seat beside the brooding cowboy. Her plain companion sat on the other side of her. In less than a minute, a man sashayed up to the prettier girl and asked her to dance.

She bounced out of her seat and led the way to the dance floor, the cowboy following.

Lacey's dark cowboy glanced up briefly from his beer, his gaze going to the pretty girl's not-as-pretty friend.

The woman sat facing the dancing, and heaved a sigh, a smile plastered to her face, her toe tapping to the beat of the music.

Lacey placed her order with Libby and made another pass through the saloon, delivering full glasses and collecting empties. When she returned to the bar, the pretty girl was just sitting down when another cowboy asked her to dance.

Off she went again, leaving her friend at the bar.

Lacey's heart went out to the girl. She wasn't exactly pretty, but she had a nice smile and just a few extra pounds.

All the while Lacey took and delivered orders, she watched the bar, the cowboy and the women beside him.

After the fourth time the skinny woman left her chunkier friend alone to dance with another cowboy, the dark-haired cowboy pushed back from the bar and stood, a frown creasing his forehead, the first change to his expression since Lacey had started watching the man.

He half-bowed, saying something to the sunny-faced big girl.

Her eyes lit up and she hopped off her barstool, lighter on her feet than Lacey would have thought.

The cowboy held out his arm, she took it, her smile widening as he led her to the dance floor. They took off in a lively two-step.

Lacey's heart lightened for the girl, and then she frowned.

Damn. Kendall had been right. The brooding cowboy *was* nice. While all the other cowboys had passed the girl by, the dark-eyed one asked her to dance, giving her the thrill of her life.

When the song ended, the cowboy returned her to her seat and bowed over her hand, thanked her and pressed a kiss to her knuckles.

The woman's face flushed a pretty pink and she batted her eyes.

Double damn. Lacey had wanted to count him off as another pretty boy, all looks, no substance, and he'd proved her wrong.

Not long after, the women left and the man returned to his beer.

He'd been there for over an hour and Lacey hadn't flirted with him once. Unusual for Lacey who'd shucked inhibitions when she'd filed for divorce. Still, the opportunity had passed and flirting now would be a little too late and awkward.

It being a weeknight, the saloon closed at midnight, patrons filtering out one by one until the only customer left was the cowboy at the bar. Lacey had let him sit there even after the saloon closed because he was handsome, he'd made a girl's night and he looked as lonely as she felt. But the place was clean and the others would want to hit the road. No matter how good looking and nice, he had to leave.

Lacey sighed and leaned against the counter. "Sorry, cowboy, the bar is closed."

He glanced up, his brown eyes so dark they looked black in the dim lighting. "I didn't realize…" The man stood, settled his cowboy hat on his head and turned to leave.

"You can come back tomorrow," Lacey offered. "It beats spending your evening alone…" she added beneath her breath.

His gaze captured hers and a smile quirked the corners of his lips. "Might just do that, and you're right—it beats being alone." The cowboy tipped his hat and left.

What was wrong with her tonight? Normally, Lacey would have flirted with the stranger and teased a smile out of him. But something had stopped her. Perhaps it was the way he'd kept to himself as if he wanted to be alone in a room full of people. More likely she'd steered clear because he was too good looking for his own good or hers. She had a hard time resisting a handsome face.

As her cowboy departed, Lacey sighed. So much for making it an interesting night. Instead of a one-night stand with a sexy hunk, she'd be going home to her empty apartment building.

"Place is clean enough. You ladies go home." Audrey Anderson, owner of the Ugly Stick Saloon, stood on her tiptoes, shoved the last bottle of whiskey onto the glass shelf behind the bar and lifted her strawberry-blond hair off the back of her neck. "Holy cow. Could it get any hotter? I can't wait to get home to a cool shower."

"And a hot cowboy?" Lacey quipped.

Jackson Gray Wolf was one of the hottest Kiowa cowboys in the county, next to his twin brothers, Mark and Luke.

Audrey had sampled all three and only hinted at how great they were, before she claimed the oldest, Jackson. "He is pretty hot, isn't he?" Audrey grinned.

"Yeah." Lacey sighed, her mind on the last cowboy to leave the bar.

Audrey had Jackson waiting for her at home. Kendall had Ed Judson. Libby had Mark and Luke Gray Wolf and Isabella had the O'Brien brothers. Which left Lacey where?

Alone.

Lacey straightened her shoulders. Alone was better than married to an ass, which her ex had been.

"You gonna be all right?" Kendall Mason slipped an arm around Lacey's waist and squeezed. "I feel like I'm deserting you, leaving you all alone in the apartment building, and all."

Lacey pasted a smile on her face and hugged her friend. "Just remember, if you and Ed ever need a third to keep the sex education lessons rolling, I'm your gal." The offer was only superficial. Though she'd had sex with Kendall and Ed, she didn't want to cause any strife between the pair. They were perfect for each other all on their own.

"I'll keep that in mind." Kendall tugged the apron over her head and hung it on a hook. "I'm serious. You should stop by on your way home."

"No, sweetie. I wouldn't dream of horning in on your first night alone with Ed in your new house. Besides, Cory McBride is supposed to have moved into the apartment below mine today." Lacey smoothed a hand over her hair. "I need to give him a proper welcome."

"Lacey." Kendall shook her head. "Just remember, he's only twenty-one. A baby."

"Like you?" Lacey's lips quirked upward. "Old enough to be legal and young enough to have plenty of stamina. Besides, I'm only twenty-eight. Hardly a hag."

"You're by no means a hag. But don't scare the poor boy. We need him here on Ladies' Night. He draws a big crowd and he needs the tips to help pay for college. Come to think of it, I haven't seen him date any of the women who hang out at the bar. He might not be into girls."

"Hot damn." Lacey clapped her hands together and rubbed them. "A challenge."

Kendall frowned. "I should have kept my mouth shut."

"Don't worry, Kendall, sweetheart. I won't wear the boy out…much." Lacey plumped her breasts and tugged up her cutoff jeans, showing a little more of her rounded derrière. "From the way the child dances, I'm sure he wouldn't mind a little more exercise. If he swings the other way, well then, no harm, no foul."

"Lacey, you crack me up. When are you going to find a man and settle down?"

Lacey's smile faded. "Honey, been there, done that, have scars to prove it. I'm thinking I might go for a woman next time. I have to admit, you were pretty damned tempting."

Kendall blushed. "You know that if I wasn't so into Ed, I'd be all over you."

"Thanks, hon, but you're the commitment type. You'd have me running screaming in the other direction. I'm all about having fun and no strings. You know me. Keep me hot and horny and the old biddies' tongues a-waggin' and I'm happy." After the women of the Temptation Garden Club had snubbed her, she loved yanking their chains. Her chest still ached when she thought about how cruel they'd been to her when she'd been in the right to divorce her cheating ex-husband.

Kendall patted Lacey's arm. "Someday you'll have to get over what those old biddies did to you. They aren't worth gettin' your dander up over."

"I know. It still galls me that they were supposed to be my friends." Lacey sucked in a deep breath and pasted a smile on her face. "I'm fine now. Even better with the friends I've made at the Ugly Stick."

"Well, the offer's open if you wanna come over."

"Thanks, sweetie." Lacey's eyes misted.

"What happened with the cute cowboy at the bar?" Kendall waggled her brows. "With a little encouragement, he might have escorted you home."

"I didn't have time to flirt."

"Ha! You always flirt." Kendall crossed her arms.

Lacey shrugged. "He had a *do not disturb* sign written across his forehead."

"That never stopped you." Kendall's eyes narrowed. "You really aren't on your game."

"Go home." Lacey waved her hands at her friend. "Ed's bound to be naked waiting at the door for you."

Kendall grinned. "Yeah, he did that our last night in the apartment. God, he was cute. Guess I'd better get home before some ho bag finds him first." She hugged Lacey and sprinted out the back.

Lacey left before Audrey could corner her and give her the third degree about why she'd walked around all night down-in-the mouth and glum. Kendall and Ed's move from the apartment house to their new home had her in a funk so blue she couldn't seem to climb out. The empty apartment house reminded her of how alone she really was in Temptation, Texas.

Her foot barely tapped the gas as she crept home to the empty house. Not until she pulled into the drive and parked next to Cory's convertible did she remember that she wouldn't be alone, if the new neighbor was still awake. And if the light burning in the window downstairs and the jumble of empty boxes stacked on the front porch were any indication, Cory was still up. If she hurried she could pop a frozen pizza in the microwave and be back down before he called it a night.

Cory was a little young for her, but any company tonight was better than going back to her apartment and being alone. Later, she'd break out her vibrator and satisfy that itch that had been growing since she'd let the hot cowboy at the bar go without coming on to him.

ABOUT THE AUTHOR

Twenty years of livin' and lovin' on a South Texas ranch raising horses, cattle, goats, ostriches and emus left an indelible impression on Myla Jackson, one she likes to instill in her red-hot stories. Myla pens wildly sexy, fun adventures of all genres including historical westerns, medieval tales, romantic suspense, contemporary romance and paranormal beasties of all shapes and sexy sizes. She lives in the tree-covered hills of Northwest Arkansas with her husband of more than 20 years and her muses—the human-wanna-be canines—Chewy and Sweetpea.

To learn more about Myla Jackson and her alter ego Elle James visit:

www.mylajackson.com

mylajackson@mylajackson.com

Boots & the Wishes (#10)

Boots & Twisters (#11)

Boots & the Bachelor (#12)

Boots & The Rogue (#13)

Boots & The Heartbreaker (#14)

Boots & Wings (#15)